BLACK WIDOW (2014) #4
writer NATHAN EDMONDSON
artist PHIL NOTO
letterer VC's CLAYTON COWLES
cover art PHIL NOTO
editor ELLIE PYLE

SHE-HULK (2014) #4
writer CHARLES SOULE
artist JAVIER PULIDO
color artist MUNTSA VICENTE
letterer VC's CLAYTON COWLES
cover art KEVIN WADA
assistant editor FRANKIE JOHNSON
editors JEANINE SCHAEFER
& TOM BRENNAN

CAPTAIN MARVEL (2014) #4
writer KELLY SUE DeCONNICK
artist DAVID LOPEZ
color artist LEE LOUGHRIDGE
letterer VC's JOE CARAMAGNA
cover art DAVID LOPEZ
assistant editor DEVIN LEWIS
editor SANA AMANAT
senior editor NICK LOWE

MS. MARVEL (2014) #4
writer G. WILLOW WILSON
artist ADRIAN ALPHONA
color artist IAN HERRING
letterer VC's JOE CARAMAGNA
cover art JAMIE McKELVIE &
MATTHEW WILSON
assistant editor DEVIN LEWIS
editor SANA AMANAT
senior editor NICK LOWE

THOR (2014) #4
writer JASON AARON
artist RUSSELL DAUTERMAN
color artist MATTHEW WILSON
letterer VC's JOE SABINO
cover art RUSSELL DAUTERMAN &
MATTHEW WILSON
assistant editor JON MOISAN
editor WIL MOSS

THE UNBEATABLE SQUIRREL GIRL (2015A) #4
writer RYAN NORTH
artist ERICA HENDERSON
color artist RICO RENZI
letterer VC's CLAYTON COWLES
cover art ERICA HENDERSON
assistant editor JON MOISAN
editor WIL MOSS
executive editor TOM BREVOORT

collection editor JENNIFER GRÜNWALD
associate editor SARAH BRUNSTAD
associate managing editor ALEX STARBUCK
editor, special projects MARK D. BEAZLEY
vp, production & special projects JEFF YOUNGQUIST
svp print, sales & marketing DAVID GABRIEL
book designer ADAM DEL RE

editor in chief AXEL ALONSO
chief creative officer JOE QUESADA
publisher DAN BUCKLEY
executive producer ALAN FINE

A-FORCE PRESENTS VOL. 4. Contains material originally published in magazine form as BLACK WIDOW #4, CAPTAIN MARVEL #4, MS. MARVEL #4, SHE-HULK #4, THOR #4 and THE UNBEATABLE SQUIRREL GIRL #4. First printing 2016. ISBN# 978-0-7851-9533-7. Published by MARVEL WORLDWIDE, INC., a subsidiary of MARVEL ENTERTAINMENT, LLC. OFFICE OF PUBLICATION: 135 West 50th Street, New York, NY 10020. **Printed in Canada.** ALAN FINE, President, Marvel Entertainment; DAN BUCKLEY, President, TV, Publishing & Brand Management; JOE QUESADA, Chief Creative Officer; TOM BREVOORT, SVP of Publishing; DAVID BOGART, SVP of Business Affairs & Operations, Publishing & Partnership; C.B. CEBULSKI, VP of Brand Management & Development, Asia; DAVID GABRIEL, SVP of Sales & Marketing, Publishing; JEFF YOUNGQUIST, VP of Production & Special Projects; DAN CARR, Executive Director of Publishing Technology; ALEX MORALES, Director of Publishing Operations; SUSAN CRESPI, Production Manager; STAN LEE, Chairman Emeritus. For information regarding advertising in Marvel Comics or on Marvel.com, please contact Vit DeBellis, Integrated Sales Manager, at vdebellis@marvel.com. For Marvel subscription inquiries, please call 888-511-5480. **Manufactured between 2/5/2016 and 3/14/2016 by SOLISCO PRINTERS, SCOTT, QC, CANADA.**

10 9 8 7 6 5 4 3 2 1

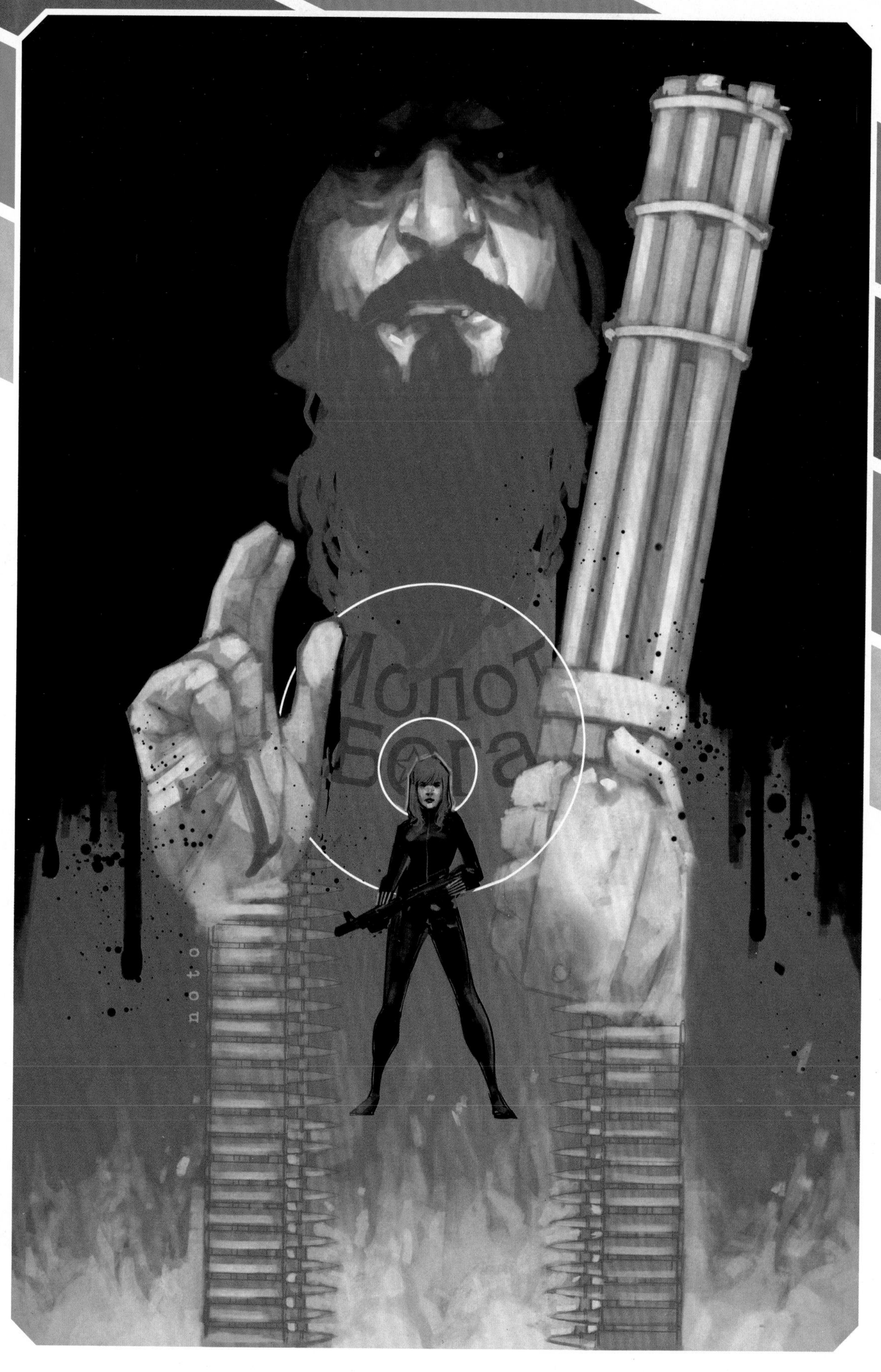

BLACK WIDOW #4

NATASHA ROMANOVA IS AN AVENGER, AN AGENT OF S.H.I.E.L.D. AND AN EX-KGB ASSASSIN, BUT ON HER OWN TIME, SHE USES HER UNIQUE SKILL SET TO ATONE FOR HER PAST. SHE IS:

BLACK WIDOW

"PUBLIC ENEMY"

NATHAN EDMONDSON
WRITER

PHIL NOTO
ARTIST

VC's CLAYTON COWLES
LETTERER & PRODUCTION

ELLIE PYL
EDITOR

AXEL ALONSO
EDITOR IN CHIEF

JOE QUESADA
CHIEF CREATIVE OFFICER

DAN BUCKLEY
PUBLISHER

ALAN FINE
EXEC. PRODUCER

THEY ARE DANGEROUS.
WE HAVE TO TAKE CARE OF THEM BEFORE IT'S TOO LATE.
THEY HAVE SINNED.

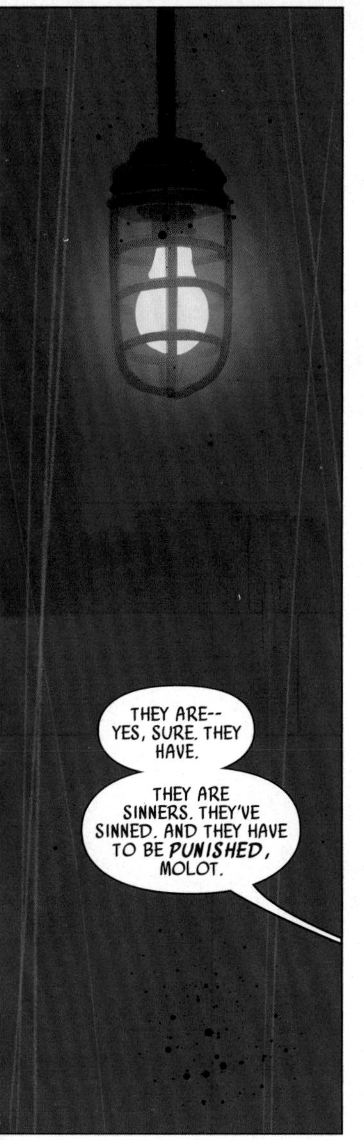
THEY ARE-- YES, SURE. THEY HAVE.
THEY ARE SINNERS. THEY'VE SINNED. AND THEY HAVE TO BE PUNISHED, MOLOT.

YOUR WORD IS LIKE FIRE TO ME. I SHALL BE YOUR HAMMER THAT BREAKS THE ROCK INTO PIECES.
...
OKAY. GOOD. JUST, MOLOT...

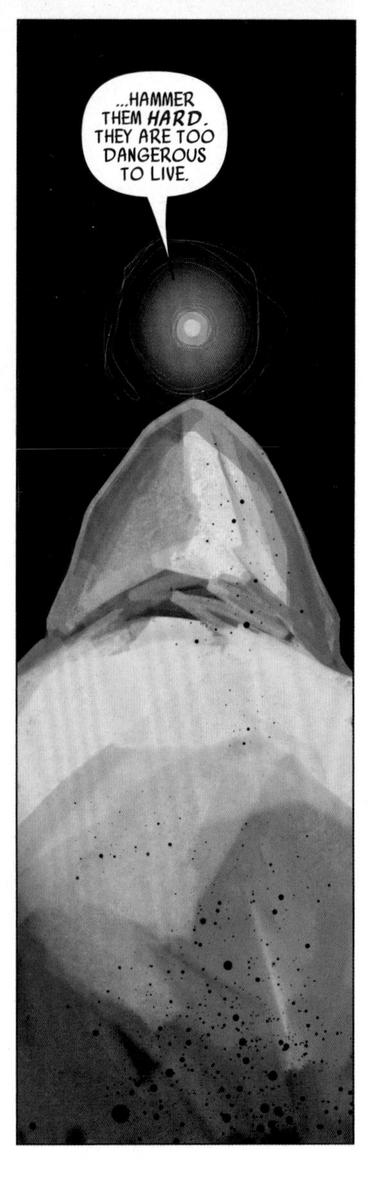
...HAMMER THEM HARD. THEY ARE TOO DANGEROUS TO LIVE.

WORKING FOR S.H.I.E.L.D. PAYS NEXT TO NOTHING.

BUT AT LEAST, SOMETIMES, IT'S TOTALLY BORING.
THE HEAD OF SECURITY WILL MEET YOU INSIDE, AGENT ROMANOFF. YOU'RE A SECURITY CONSULTANT, HERE TO SELL A NEW MOTION SENSOR SYSTEM.
PLANT THE BUGS, LEARN WHAT YOU CAN.

UH-HUH. ANY IDEA WHAT KIND OF "MOTION SENSOR SYSTEM"?
I THINK THERE'S SOME INFORMATION IN THE BROCHURES IN THERE.

TR-590 MOTION SENSOR SYSTEM
OH, SUPER.
GOOD LUCK, AGENT ROMANOFF.
PLEASE, JUST CALL ME "NUMBER 25225."

BORING.
BEST TO REMEMBER THAT S.H.I.E.L.D. IS A BUREAUCRACY. WHEN YOU START TO ARGUE, YOU ONLY GET TANGLED UP IN RED TAPE.

BUT THEY'RE BETTER THAN THE OTHER DIRECT-ACTION, COVERT-INTEL BUREAUCRACIES. USUALLY.
ONCE YOU'VE FOUGHT OFF INVADING ALIENS FOR THEM, SOMETIMES DOING S.H.I.E.L.D.'S GROUND-LEVEL WORK CAN BE TEDIOUS.

BUT THE TRUTH ABOUT INTELLIGENCE GATHERING? THE DEVIL IS IN THE DETAILS.

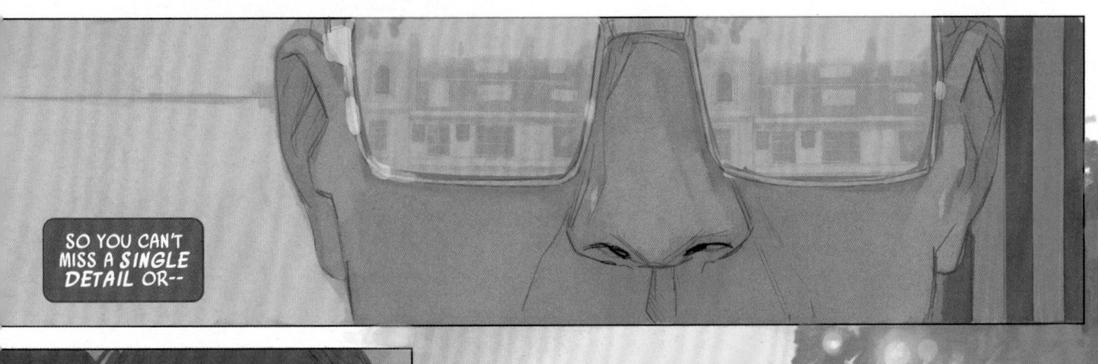
SO YOU CAN'T MISS A SINGLE DETAIL OR--

YOU MIGHT MISS THE DEVIL HIMSELF...

RO

OM!

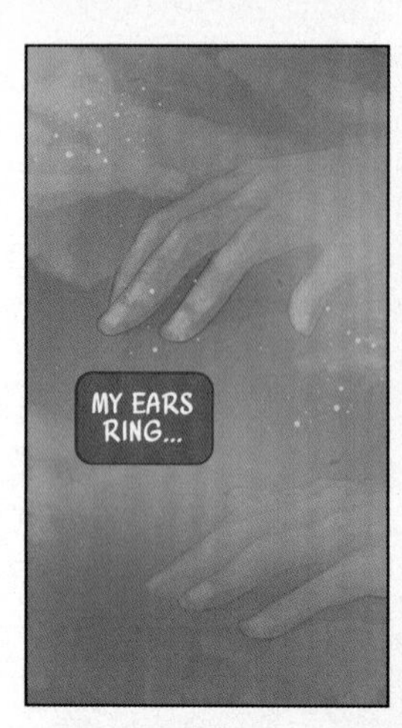
MY EARS RING...

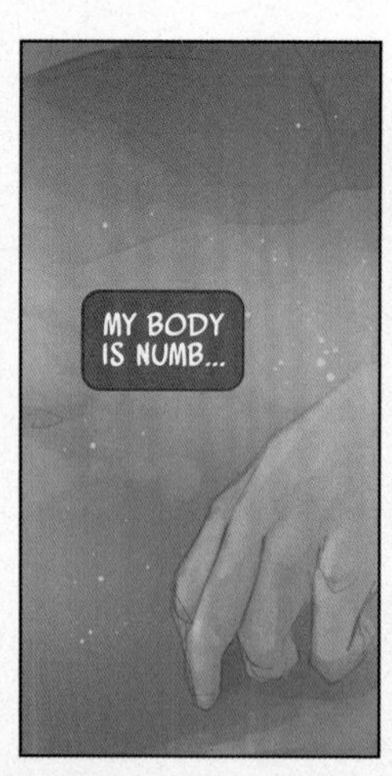
MY BODY IS NUMB...

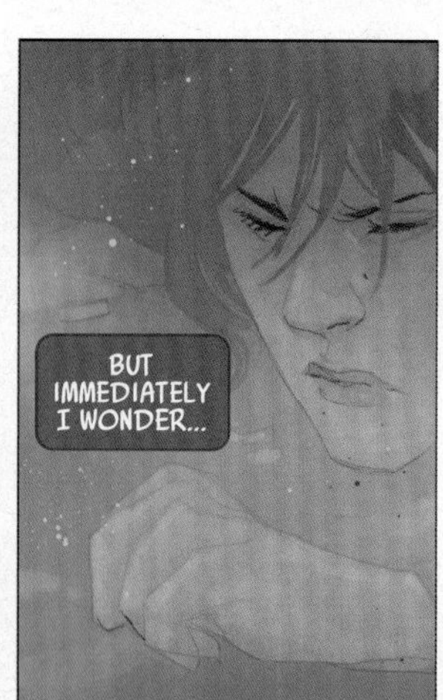
BUT IMMEDIATELY I WONDER...

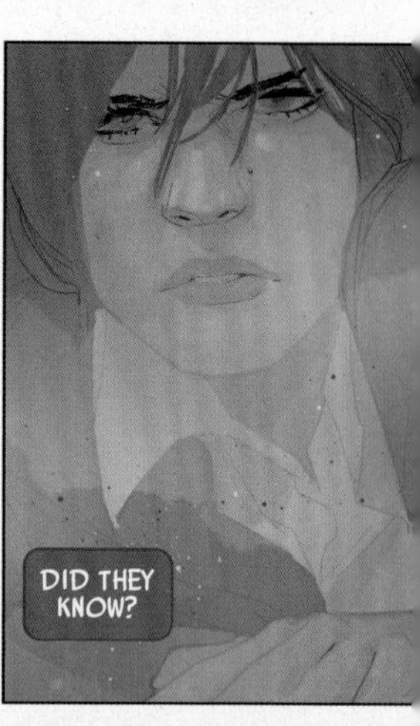
DID THEY KNOW?

AGENT ROMANOFF!
CALL DIRECTOR HILL! *I'M IN PURSUIT.*

WHOEVER HE IS, HE'S A *COWARD*.

AND I'VE GOT HIM.

WHERE DID YOU GO?

сюда.

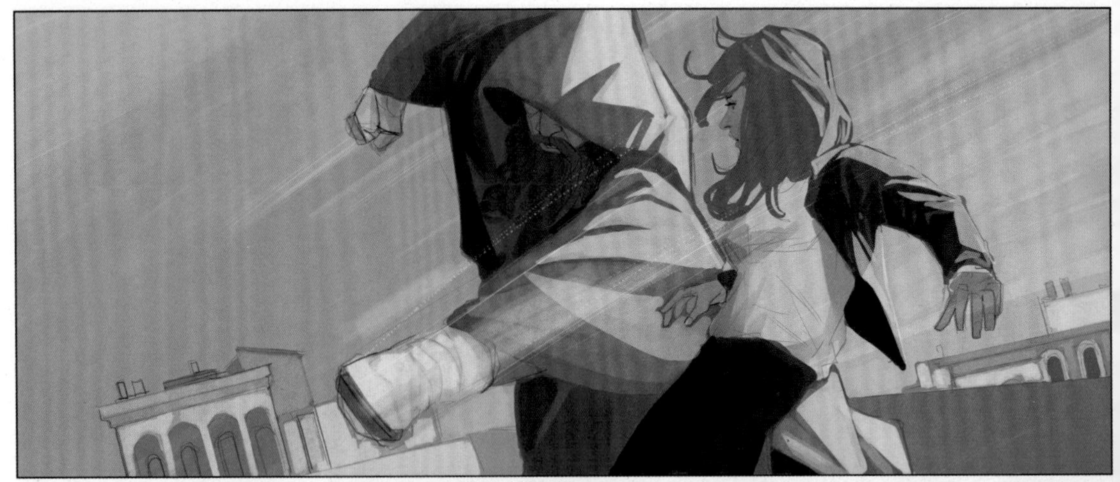

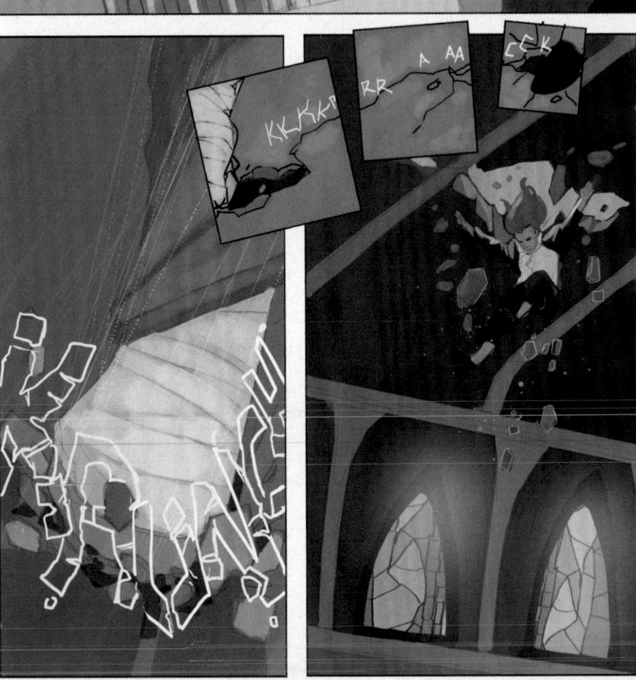

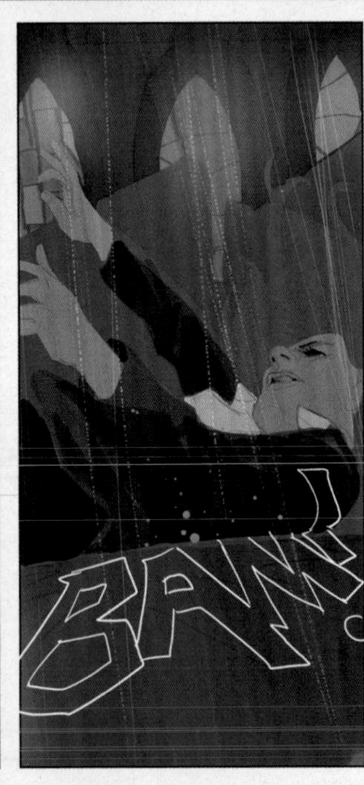
BAM!

YEP, BORING.

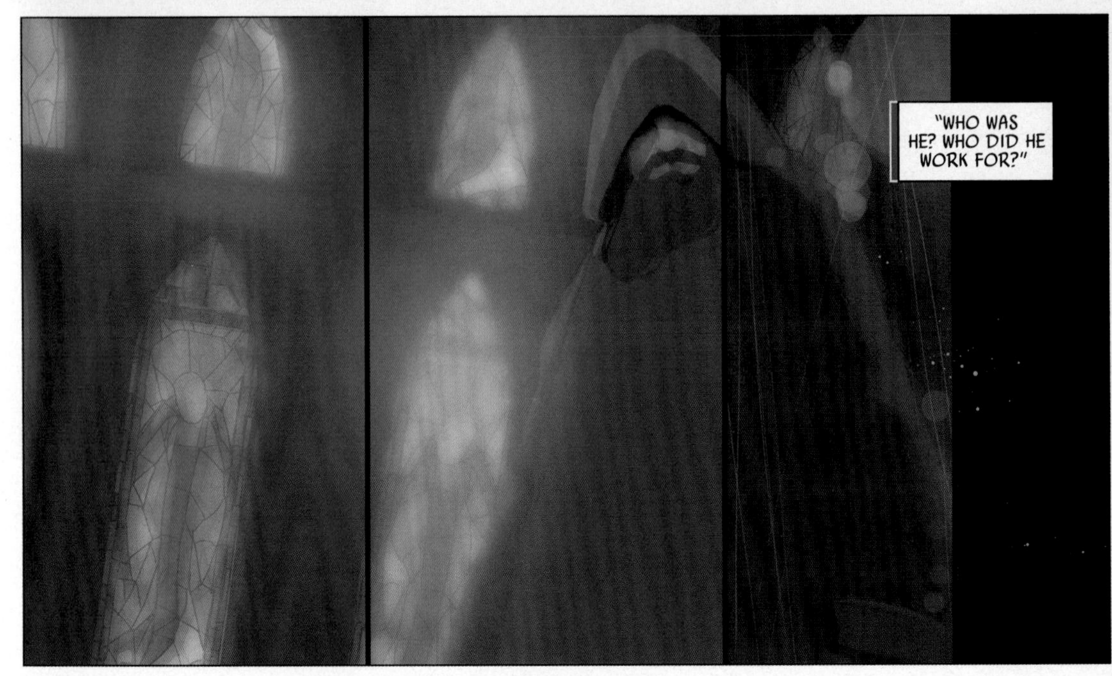
"WHO WAS HE? WHO DID HE WORK FOR?"

ALL I KNOW IS HE IS RUSSIAN, DIRECTOR. I COULD NOT EVEN TELL YOU FROM WHAT REGION. HE ONLY SAID ONE WORD.

HE BLEW UP THE ENTIRE EMBASSY...
THEY ARE MAKING A STATEMENT, BUT TO WHOM? AND...

WHO ARE THEY? "FEAR THE CHAOS." WHAT DOES THAT EVEN MEAN?
WE NEED TO QUESTION THE AMBASSADOR'S PEOPLE.
WE CAN'T. THEY'VE DENIED US ACCESS.
WHY?

THAT IS AN INTERESTING QUESTION. AND ONE THAT S.H.I.E.L.D. NEEDS ANSWERED.
...SO, HOW CAN YOU MANAGE WITH THE ARM?

I CAN MANAGE.
GOOD. BECAUSE WE NEED YOU TO GET SOME ANSWERS...

WITHOUT ASKING ANY QUESTIONS.

CABINET OF MINISTERS.
KIEV, UKRAINE.
A DISCONNECTED, BLOODY TRAIL...

SHADOW WARFARE, POLITICAL TARGETS...
BZZZZ

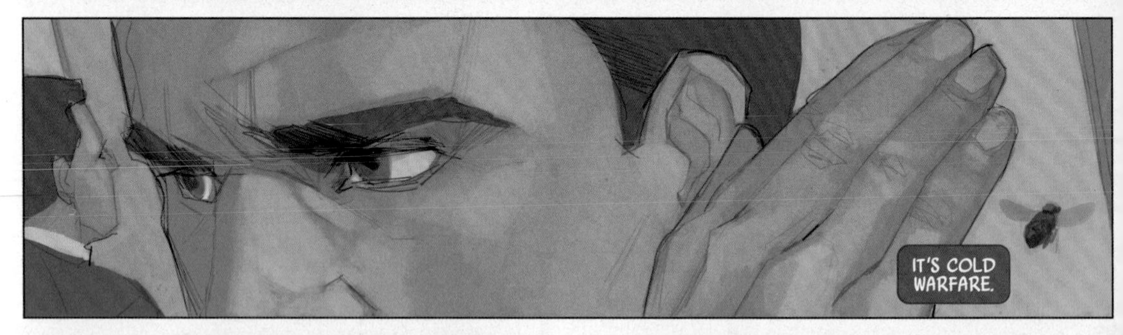
IT'S COLD WARFARE.

BUT NO ONE TOLD ME THERE WAS ANOTHER COLD WAR.
...IT'S A PROBLEM WE MUST SOLVE. THAT IS WHY.
THE PROBLEM DIED WITH THE AMBASSADOR!

YOU KNOW WHAT HE WAS INVOLVED IN, AND YOU KNOW WHAT THEY ARE CAPABLE OF! IT WILL NOT END WITH HIM.
HE SAID CHAOS WOULD FOLLOW.
YES, YES, WE'VE HEARD IT ALL BEFORE. BUT THIS MAN IS NOT INDESTRUCTIBLE. IF WE SEND A TEAM AFTER HIM...

IF THE TEAM FAILS?

WELL. WHAT DO YOU RECOMMEND?
WHAT THIS MOLOT BOGA DID CONSTITUTES AN ACT OF WAR. HE BLEW UP AN EMBASSY. THIS IS NOT PERSONAL, IT IS A NATIONAL--
HE IS A HITMAN. NOTHING MORE. AND FROM WHAT WE HEAR--
--HIS NEXT TARGET IS THE CROATIAN AMBASSADOR; HE'S IN CAPE TOWN THIS WEEK AND--
WE DO NOT GO AFTER MOLOT. LET HIM CLEAN UP THIS EMBARRASSING MESS SO NONE OF IT CAN BE CONNECTED BACK TO THE AMBASSADOR.
HE HAS CAUSED US ENOUGH DAMAGE ALREADY.
"MARIA--
"IT APPEARS THE EMBASSY BOMBING WAS A HIT. A HIT ON ONE MAN."
"ONE MAN? THAT'S HEAVY-HANDED."
"IT IS."
"WHAT'S NEXT?"
"ANOTHER TARGET. SOUTH AFRICA."
"GOOD. USE THE S.H.I.E.L.D. CREDIT CARD, BOOK A FLIGHT--"
"WAY AHEAD OF YOU."

CAPE TOWN.
DRIVER, WE CAN GO.
ONE BENEFIT OF GOVERNMENT WORK? FREQUENT FLYER MILES.
SERIOUSLY, I GET BUMPED UP ABOUT EVERY FLIGHT. STILL NOT AS NICE AS THE DIRECTOR'S PRIVATE JET THOUGH...
ESPECIALLY WHEN YOU'RE IN A RUSH...
...AS DIPLOMATICALLY PROTECTED BAGS FULL OF SPY EQUIPMENT ALWAYS CAUSE DELAYS.
AND RIGHT NOW, I AM DELAYED. AND I'M AFRAID OF WHAT I MIGHT BE LATE FOR.

WHAT'S HAPPENING UP THERE?
NOT SURE, MR. AMBASSADOR-- THERE'S SOMEONE IN THE ROAD.

"WELL DRIVE AROUND HIM! WE'RE RUNNING LATE AS IT IS."
"IT'S A BIT OF A JAM, SIR."
CLEANSE ME, FOR I HAVE NEVER DONE ANYTHING GOOD IN YOUR SIGHT.
YOU LIVEST IN THE HIGHEST AND CAREST FOR THE HUMBLE...
LOOK UPON YOUR SERVANT.
OH MY GOD.
BRTRTRTRT
RTRTRTRT

CHIK
HE IN WHOM THERE IS NO CHANGE NOR SHADOW OF VARIATION...
BANISH FROM ME, THY LOWLY AND WRETCHED SERVANT, ALL--
BHOOM
SOMEHOW I THINK GOD CANNOT HEAR YOUR PRAYERS, MONK--
THAT IS, OVER THE SOUND OF YOUR HUGE ASS MACHINE GUN.
DO NOT INTERRUPT THE RIGHTEOUS WORK OF THE HAMMER OF GOD--
BRINGING HIM IN ALIVE MAY NOT BE AN OPTION.
BRTRTRTRTRTRTRTRTRT
HAMMER THIS.

KABAM!

...KILLING HIM MIGHT NOT BE AN OPTION EITHER.
ESPECIALLY WITH ONE BUSTED ARM.

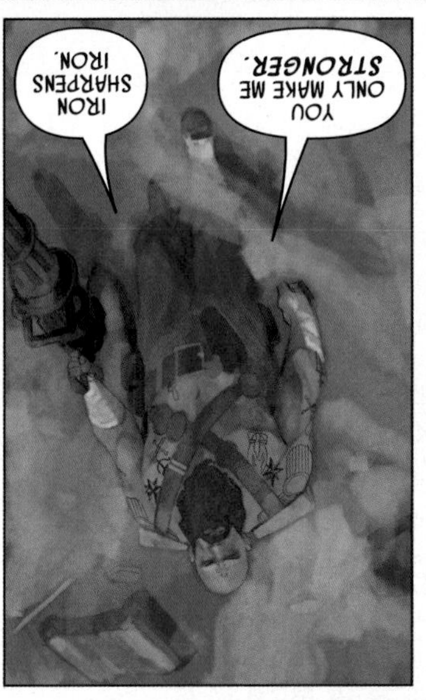
YOU ONLY MAKE ME *STRONGER*.
IRON SHARPENS IRON.

THE TOOL OF THE ALMIGHTY DOES NOT DULL, DOES NOT RUST--

THE THING ABOUT LEAD-SPITTING WEAPONS--

--THEY EVENTUALLY RUN OUT OF *LEAD*.
(UNLIKE ALIEN PLASMA WEAPONS OR LASERS OR WHATEVER.)
CHING CHA CHING CHA CHING

WELL...HE HAS TO RUN OUT *SOMETIME*, RIGHT?

CLIK
CLIK
AH, THERE WE GO.

BLAM
BLAM
BLAM
IT'S TWO AGAINST NONE NOW, PAL. STAND DOWN OR I SHOOT--
BLAM
BLAM
BLAM

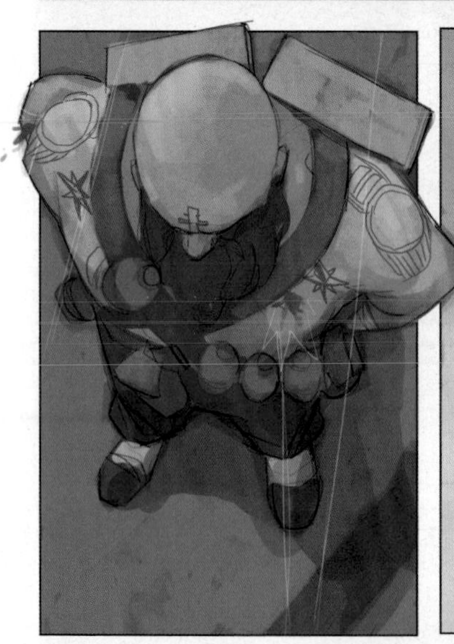

TWO AND ALSO TWO.

BLAM

AMAZING WHAT COMES TO MIND IN THE HEAT OF THE MOMENT: I CAN'T HELP BUT THINK THAT SO MUCH ABOUT THIS IS ALL, ALL WRONG.
I'M A SPY. NOT SOME ROOFTOP-JUMPING ARCHER, SHIELD-WIELDING SUPER-SOLDIER, OR SHINY-METAL PHILANTHROBOT.
I NEED TO MAKE THAT CLEAR ON MY BUSINESS CARD. ESPIONAGE IS SHADOW WARFARE.
CHOK
CHOK
COLD COMBAT.
DOES ANYTHING ABOUT THIS FEEL COLD TO YOU?
KA BOOM

CLEANSE US OF EVERY IMPURITY, ALMIGHTY ONE.

BAM

COUGH COUGH
SOMETIMES, I WISH THIS JOB WAS A BIT MORE BORING.

I WILL SEE THIS THROUGH.
I WILL FIND HIM.

WE CAN CALL IN THE AVENGERS.
TO WHAT EFFECT? TO CLEAN THE WRECKAGE FROM THE STREET? TEND TO THE WOUNDED? BANNER GOING TO APPLY SOME BAND-AIDS?
MARIA, NOT BECAUSE I **WANT** THE JOB, BUT YOU NEED A SPY TO TRACK THIS GUY DOWN. HE DISAPPEARED THAT EASILY BECAUSE HE HAS **SUPPORT**. I MEAN, CORRECT ME IF I'M WRONG BUT--

YES, HE HAS SUPPORT. HE GOT AWAY IN THIS. A HELICOPTER WE CAN'T IDENTIFY THAT DISAPPEARED OVER THE MOUNTAINS, HEADED NORTHEAST.
WE HAVE NO INFORMATION. WE NEED THE BEST SPY OUT THERE.

WHERE WILL YOU START?
I THINK I'LL PICK UP ONE OF THE UKRAINIANS AND ASK A FEW QUESTIONS.
AND I DON'T INTEND TO BE ALL THAT **NICE** ABOUT IT.

WHEN YOU NEED THEM, AGENTS ARE AT YOUR DISPOSAL.
AND ANY SPECIAL GEAR YOU'D LIKE?
AS A MATTER OF FACT... YES. I'LL GIVE YOU A LIST.
AND I NEED TO USE A PHONE... MINE MELTED.
YOU HAVE SOMEONE WHO CAN LOOK INTO THE HELO?
THERE IS SOMEONE. A RAVEN.

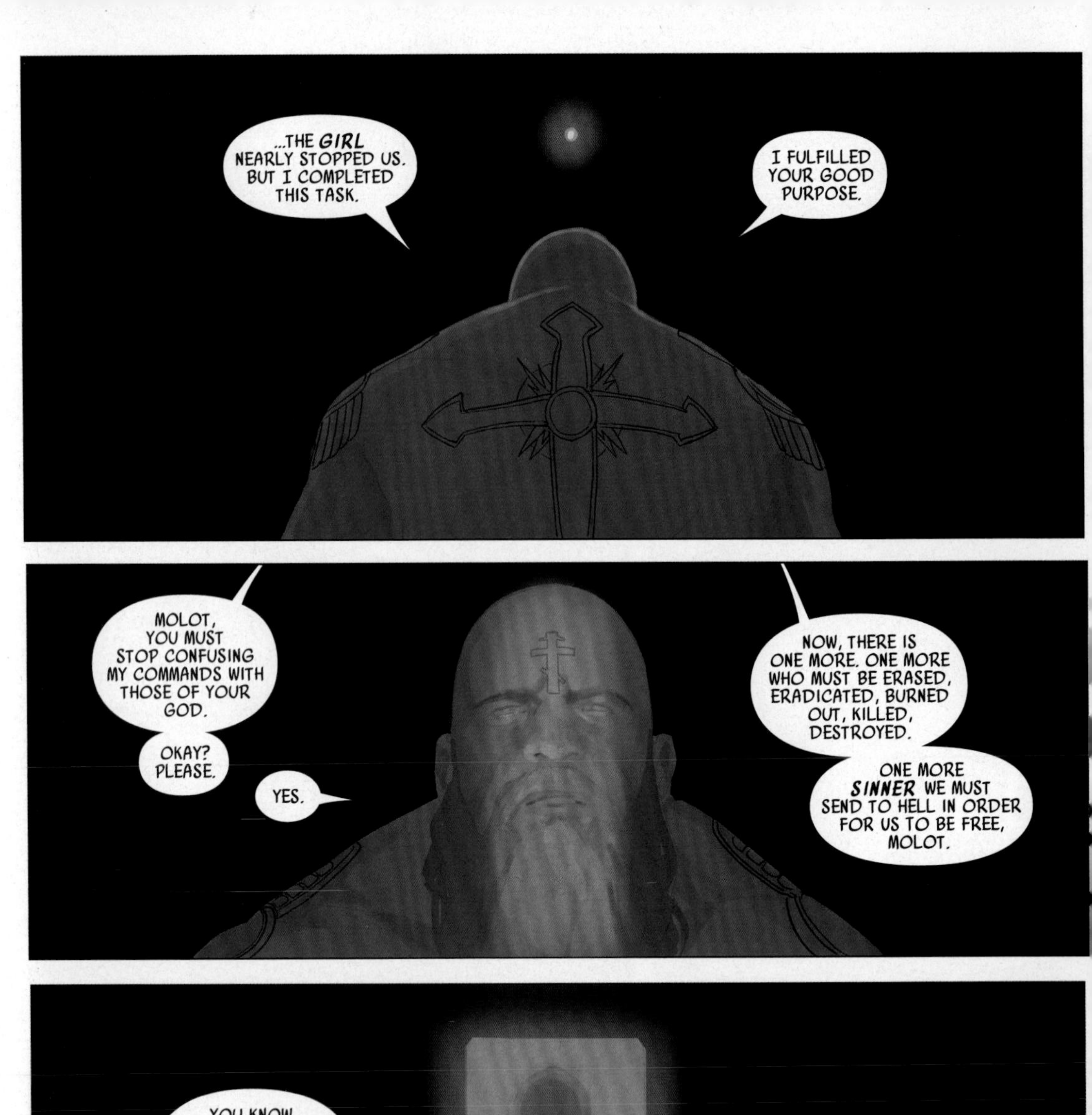
...THE GIRL NEARLY STOPPED US. BUT I COMPLETED THIS TASK.
I FULFILLED YOUR GOOD PURPOSE.
MOLOT, YOU MUST STOP CONFUSING MY COMMANDS WITH THOSE OF YOUR GOD.
OKAY? PLEASE.
YES.
NOW, THERE IS ONE MORE. ONE MORE WHO MUST BE ERASED, ERADICATED, BURNED OUT, KILLED, DESTROYED.
ONE MORE SINNER WE MUST SEND TO HELL IN ORDER FOR US TO BE FREE, MOLOT.

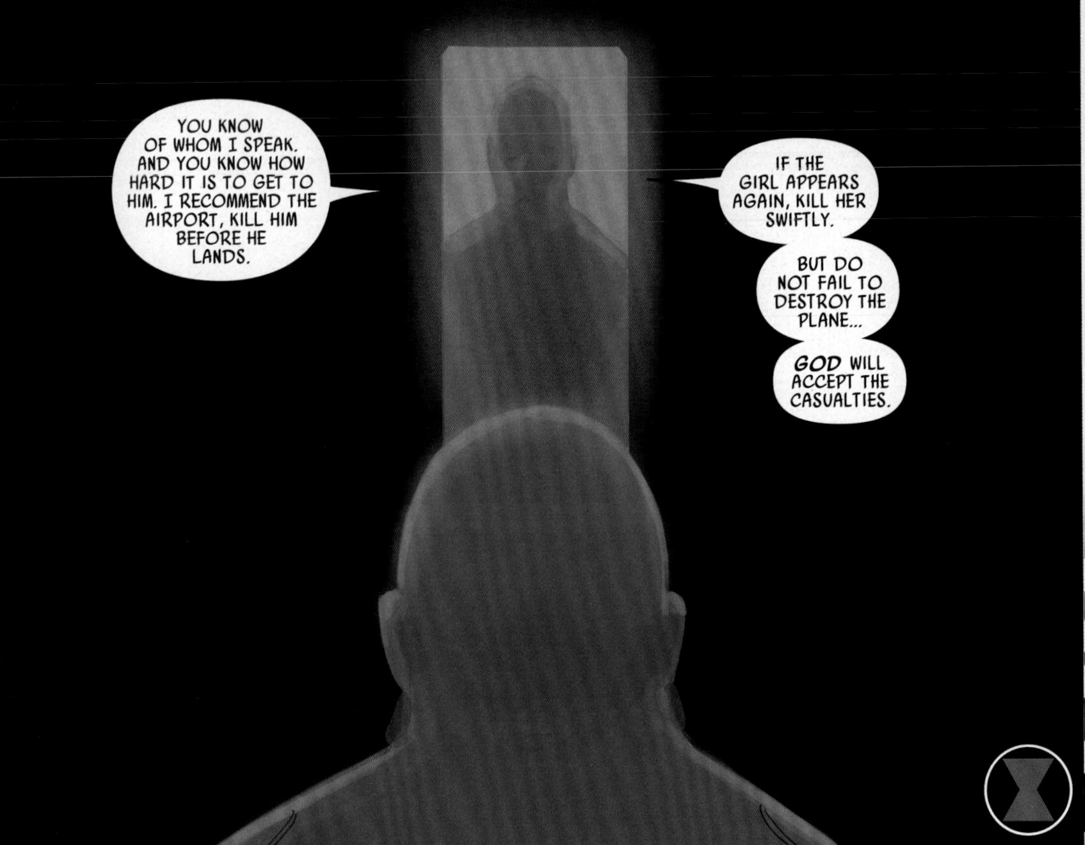
YOU KNOW OF WHOM I SPEAK. AND YOU KNOW HOW HARD IT IS TO GET TO HIM. I RECOMMEND THE AIRPORT, KILL HIM BEFORE HE LANDS.
IF THE GIRL APPEARS AGAIN, KILL HER SWIFTLY.
BUT DO NOT FAIL TO DESTROY THE PLANE...
GOD WILL ACCEPT THE CASUALTIES.

SHE-HULK #4

Jennifer Walters was a shy attorney, good at her job and quiet in her life, when she found herself gunned down by criminals. A gamma-irradiated blood transfusion from her cousin, Dr. Bruce Banner, a.k.a. the Incredible Hulk, didn't just give her a second chance at life, it gave her super strength and bulletproof green skin. Wherever justice is threatened, you'll find the Sensational...

SHE-HULK

HI, GUYS-- WELCOME BACK! SHE-HULK HERE, AND BOY DID LAST MONTH'S ISSUE END WITH A BANG. OR A DOOM, ACTUALLY.
KRISTOFF VERNARD, THE SON OF EVIL LATVERIAN DICTATOR DOCTOR DOOM, HIRED ME TO HELP HIM GET ASYLUM IN THIS COUNTRY TO GET AWAY FROM DEAR OLD DEMANDING DADDY.
ER...IT'S POSSIBLE I WAS THE ONLY LAWYER WHO SAID YES TO TAKING ON DR. DOOM, BUT DOES IT REALLY MATTER? A CLIENT'S A CLIENT, AND KRISTOFF WAS MY CLIENT.
I ADMIT HE WAS A LITTLE DIFFICULT... MAYBE A TAD ENTITLED... A BIT CONDESCENDING. ALL RIGHT, HE WAS A TOTAL JERK.
OH! I SHOULD MENTION THAT WE'VE BEEN GETTING ALL OF YOUR FABULOUS LETTERS--BUT BECAUSE SPACE IS A LITTLE TIGHT THIS MONTH, WE WON'T BE ABLE TO PUBLISH THEM QUITE YET. BUT PLEASE KEEP SENDING THEM! JUST EMAIL MHEROES@MARVEL.COM AND MARK "OK TO PRINT."
ANYWAY, BACK TO KRISTOFF.
I HAD MY WORK CUT OUT FOR ME. BUT AFTER FIGHTING DOOMBOTS, NYC TRAFFIC, AND KRISTOFF'S BLASÉ ATTITUDE, I FINALLY PRESENTED MY CASE TO THE JUDGE-- AND WON.
BUT DR. DOOM WAS PRETTY UNHAPPY ABOUT THAT--SO UNHAPPY HE SMASHED HIS WAY INTO THE COURTROOM AND KIDNAPPED KRISTOFF RIGHT OUT FROM UNDER US!

CHARLES SOULE writer
JAVIER PULIDO artist
MUNTSA VICENTE color artist
VC's CLAYTON COWLES letterer

KEVIN WADA cover artist
FRANKIE JOHNSON assistant editor
JEANINE SCHAEFER & TOM BRENNAN editors

AXEL ALONSO editor in chief
JOE QUESADA chief creative officer
DAN BUCKLEY publisher
ALAN FINE exec. producer

TAP
WANT ME TO FILE THAT, MS. WALTERS?
VERNARD, KRISTOFF
BROOKLYN, NEW YORK.
I MEAN, THAT CASE IS FINISHED, ISN'T IT?
WHEN DR. DOOM COMES AND WHISKS YOUR CLIENT--WHO HAPPENS TO BE HIS SON AND HEIR--RIGHT OUT FROM UNDER YOUR NOSE IN THE COURTROOM...
WELL, SOMETIMES YOU HAVE TO KNOW WHEN TO MOVE ON TO THE NEXT ONE.
TAP
OH, ALSO. THAT SACK OF LATVERIAN FRANCS KRISTOFF PAID US WITH? I TRIED TO EXCHANGE IT AT THE BANK. THEY CONFISCATED IT.
SAID IT WAS "CONFLICT CURRENCY"--ILLEGAL TENDER. YOU'RE LUCKY TO HAVE ANGIE HUANG AS YOUR PARALEGAL, MS. WALTERS, OR THAT COULD'VE GOTTEN STICKY.
TAP
AND THE REALLY TOUGH THING, TOO, IS THAT YOU WON. POLITICAL ASYLUM FOR KRISTOFF VERNARD, OF ALL PEOPLE. THE SON OF DOOM!
SORT OF A SHAME, REALLY... OH WELL, LIKE I SAID, YOU JUST HAVE TO KNOW WHEN TO MOVE--
TAP
KRACK
--ON.
VERNARD, KRISTOFF
I'M GOING OUT OF TOWN FOR A COUPLE DAYS, ANGIE.
OH?
YEAH. EVEN ATTORNEYS NEED LEGAL ADVICE OCCASIONALLY. YOU KNOW--

SAN FRANCISCO, CALIFORNIA.
"--SEE THINGS FROM A NEW PERSPECTIVE."
THANKS SO MUCH FOR TAKING THE TIME, MATT.
NO SWEAT, JEN. FOR A FELLOW PRACTITIONER OF THE RAREFIED ART OF SUPER HERO LAWYERING?
PROFESSIONAL COURTESY DOESN'T EVEN COVER IT. MY VERY SINCERE PLEASURE. HOW ABOUT THIS VIEW, EH?
STUNNING. JUST STUNNING.

I'LL TAKE YOUR WORD FOR IT.
OH...RIGHT. I'M SORRY, I MEAN, YOU'RE DAREDEVIL. IT'S SO EASY TO FORGET YOU'RE--
DON'T WORRY. I CAN SEE IT--JUST NOT THE WAY YOU DO.
I COME UP HERE A LOT.
GREAT PLACE TO THINK.
THE ZEALOUS ADVOCATE

A CHARLES & JAVIER SHOW
WITH
MUNTSA ON COLORS!
CLAYTON ON LETTERS!
TOM, JEANINE & FRANKIE
ON SOMETHING

MAYBE WE'VE NEVER TALKED ABOUT IT, BUT I HAVE THIS RADAR SENSE. LETS ME MAKE A MENTAL PICTURE OF THINGS AROUND ME. IT COMES IN HANDY, BUT IT CAN ALSO GET DISTRACTING.
DOWN THERE, IT'S ALL CARS, BUILDINGS, PEOPLE. UP HERE, THOUGH...
IT'S WIIIDE OPEN. I LOVE IT.

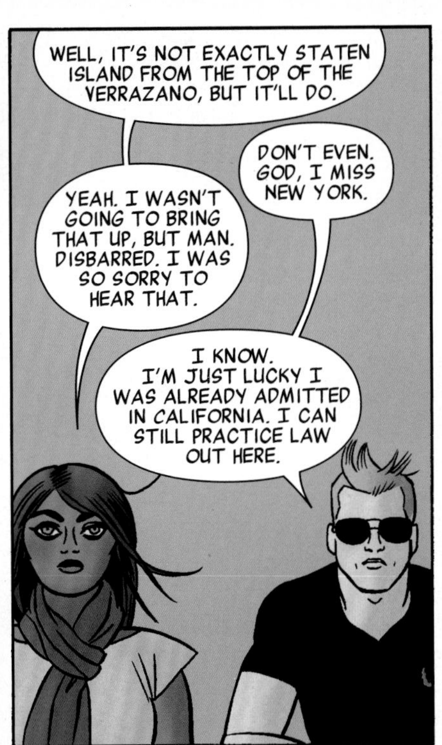
WELL, IT'S NOT EXACTLY STATEN ISLAND FROM THE TOP OF THE VERRAZANO, BUT IT'LL DO.
DON'T EVEN. GOD, I MISS NEW YORK.
YEAH. I WASN'T GOING TO BRING THAT UP, BUT MAN. DISBARRED. I WAS SO SORRY TO HEAR THAT.
I KNOW. I'M JUST LUCKY I WAS ALREADY ADMITTED IN CALIFORNIA. I CAN STILL PRACTICE LAW OUT HERE.

YOU KNOW, YOU THINK SOMETHING LIKE DISBARMENT WOULD... END YOUR LIFE, JUST DESTROY YOUR ENTIRE SENSE OF SELF. IT'S ONE THING FOR DAREDEVIL TO GET HIT WITH TERRIBLE THINGS, BUT MATT MURDOCK, ESQ....? THAT'S SUPPOSED TO BE THE STABLE PART OF MY LIFE.
YOU OKAY?
ANYWAY, THEN IT HAPPENS, AND...IT'S NO PICNIC, BUT YOU KNOW, LIFE GOES ON.

BUT YOU DIDN'T COME ALL THE WAY OUT HERE JUST TO OFFER YOUR CONDOLENCES FOR MY PROFESSIONAL CAREER. YOU SAID YOU NEEDED SOME ADVICE?
I DO.
FIRE AWAY. I'LL EVEN GIVE YOU THE FRIENDS AND FAMILY RATE.

MY LAST CLIENT WAS KRISTOFF VERNARD. YOU KNOW, DOOM'S SON?
SURE. WHAT DID HE NEED?
ASYLUM. HE WAS TRYING TO DEFECT FROM LATVERIA.
OOF. TRICKY.
YUP. BUT I WON.
WOW. GOOD WORK. I WONDER WHAT DOOM THINKS ABOUT THAT. SERVES HIM RIGHT. LATVERIA... MAN. I WAS THERE NOT LONG AGO. TERRIBLE PLACE.
I KNOW WHAT HE THINKS. HE BROKE INTO THE COURTROOM AND STOLE KRISTOFF. FLEW AWAY WITH HIM.

I CAN'T STOP THINKING ABOUT IT. KRISTOFF WAS NO PICNIC--HUGE JERK, REALLY--BUT HE'S ENTITLED TO MAKE HIS OWN CHOICES.
I GET IT. YOU'RE WONDERING IF YOU SHOULD GO AFTER HIM, AREN'T YOU?
...MAAAAAYBE?

THIS IS ALWAYS TOUGH. WE'RE LAWYERS, AND SO WE TAKE AN OATH TO BE ZEALOUS ADVOCATES FOR OUR CLIENTS--TO GO TO ANY LENGTHS TO REPRESENT THEIR INTERESTS.
BUT WE'RE ALSO SUPER HEROES, WHICH MEANS OUR "ANY LENGTHS" STRETCHES A LOT FARTHER THAN IT DOES FOR YOUR AVERAGE ATTORNEY DRAFTING WILLS IN PEORIA.
LET ME TELL YOU A STORY.

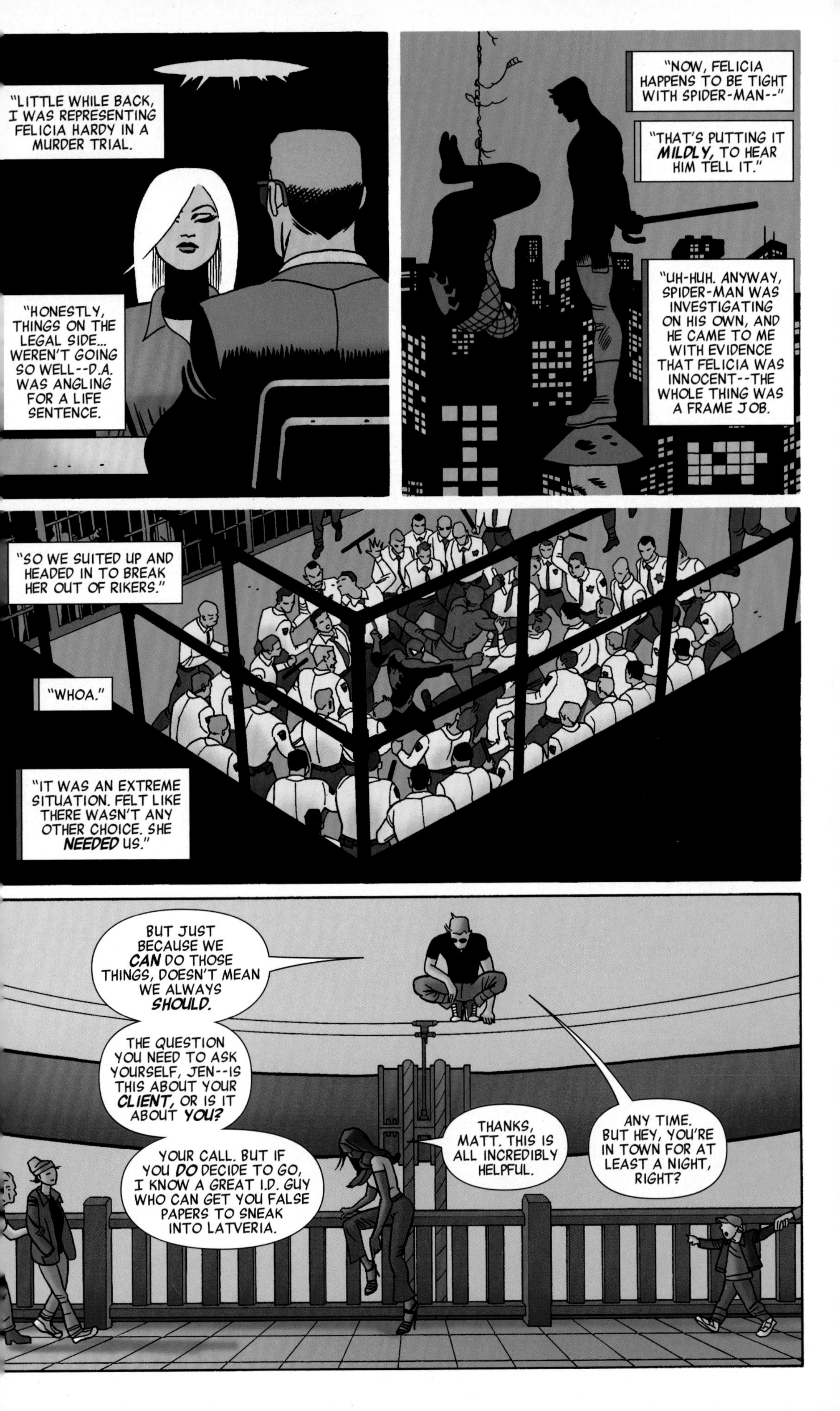
"LITTLE WHILE BACK, I WAS REPRESENTING FELICIA HARDY IN A MURDER TRIAL.
"HONESTLY, THINGS ON THE LEGAL SIDE... WEREN'T GOING SO WELL--D.A. WAS ANGLING FOR A LIFE SENTENCE.
"NOW, FELICIA HAPPENS TO BE TIGHT WITH SPIDER-MAN--"
"THAT'S PUTTING IT MILDLY, TO HEAR HIM TELL IT."
"UH-HUH. ANYWAY, SPIDER-MAN WAS INVESTIGATING ON HIS OWN, AND HE CAME TO ME WITH EVIDENCE THAT FELICIA WAS INNOCENT--THE WHOLE THING WAS A FRAME JOB.
"SO WE SUITED UP AND HEADED IN TO BREAK HER OUT OF RIKERS."
"WHOA."
"IT WAS AN EXTREME SITUATION. FELT LIKE THERE WASN'T ANY OTHER CHOICE. SHE NEEDED US."
BUT JUST BECAUSE WE CAN DO THOSE THINGS, DOESN'T MEAN WE ALWAYS SHOULD.
THE QUESTION YOU NEED TO ASK YOURSELF, JEN--IS THIS ABOUT YOUR CLIENT, OR IS IT ABOUT YOU?
YOUR CALL. BUT IF YOU DO DECIDE TO GO, I KNOW A GREAT I.D. GUY WHO CAN GET YOU FALSE PAPERS TO SNEAK INTO LATVERIA.
THANKS, MATT. THIS IS ALL INCREDIBLY HELPFUL.
ANY TIME. BUT HEY, YOU'RE IN TOWN FOR AT LEAST A NIGHT, RIGHT?

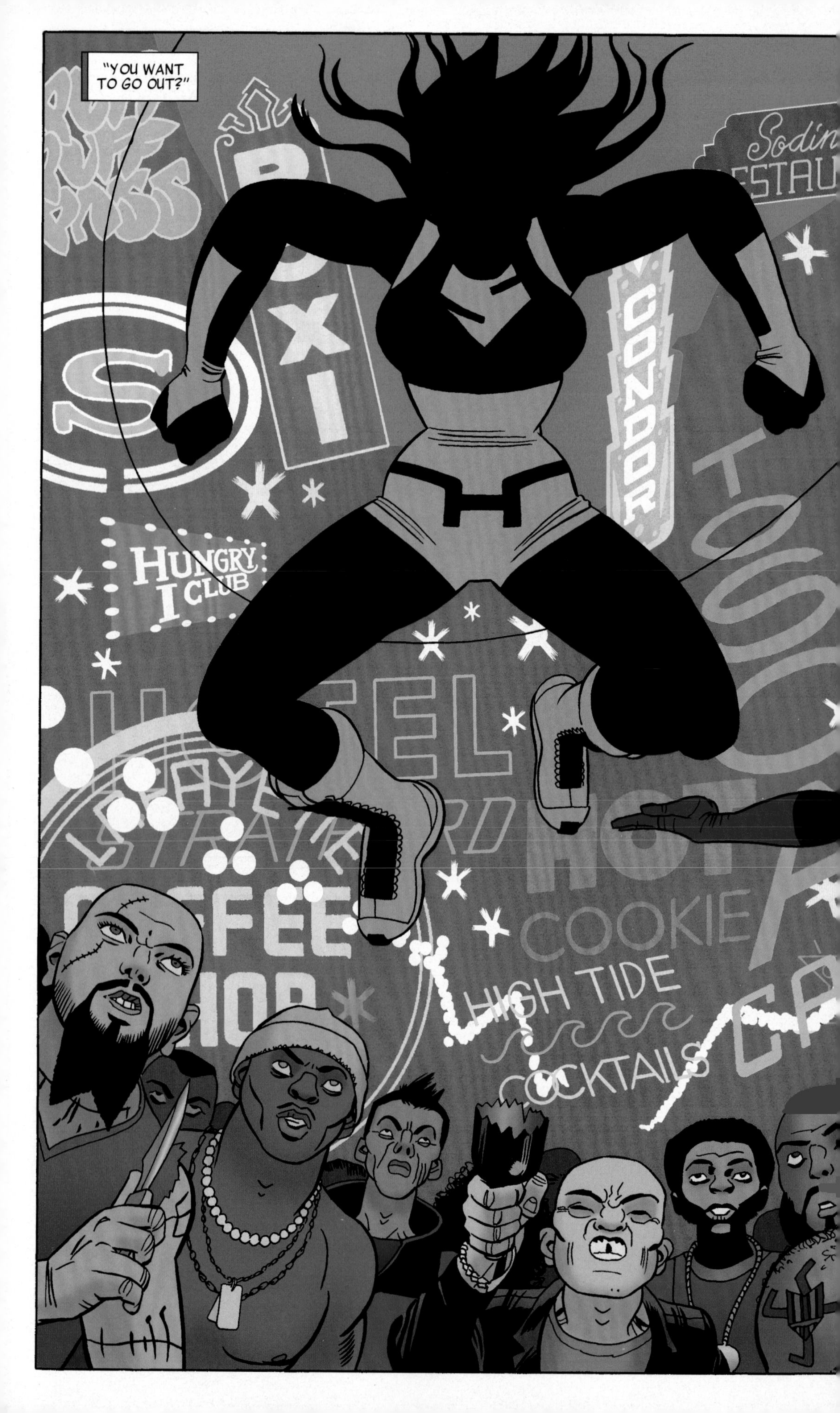
"YOU WANT TO GO OUT?"
HUNGRY I CLUB
CONDOR
COOKIE
HIGH TIDE
COCKTAILS

BEER - ICE
WINES
TOBACCOS
BROILED
BAG
BURGERS
PANTERA
KEYS
BIG AL'S
BAR
GOLDEN BOY
PIZZA

YOU EVER THINK IT'S FUNNY WE'VE NEVER GONE UP AGAINST EACH OTHER IN COURT?
NOT REALLY. LOTTA LAWYERS OUT THERE, MATT.

STILL, YOU'D THINK EVEN *ONCE.* OH WELL, MAYBE SOMEDAY.
CAREFUL WHAT YOU WISH FOR, PAL. THANK YOU, COUNSELOR.

ANY TIME, COUNSELOR. SAFE FLIGHT BACK TO BROOKLYN.
ACTUALLY...

"...I MIGHT MAKE A LITTLE DETOUR FIRST."
LATVERIAIR

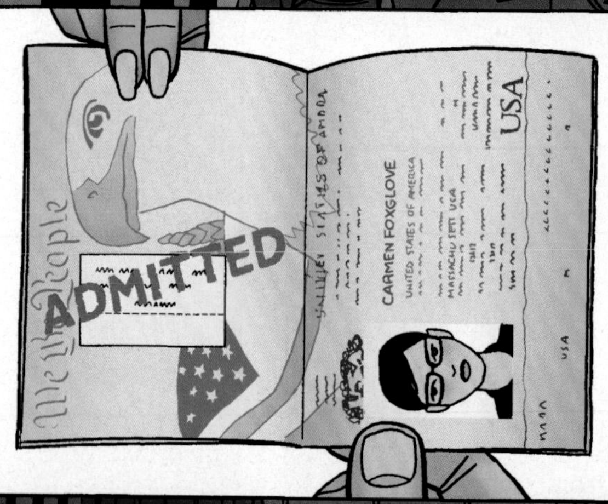
USA
CARMEN FOXGLOVE
UNITED STATES OF AMERICA
ADMITTED

DOOMSTADT, CAPITAL CITY OF LATVERIA.

OKAY... HOW EXACTLY AM I GOING TO...

THAT'LL DO.

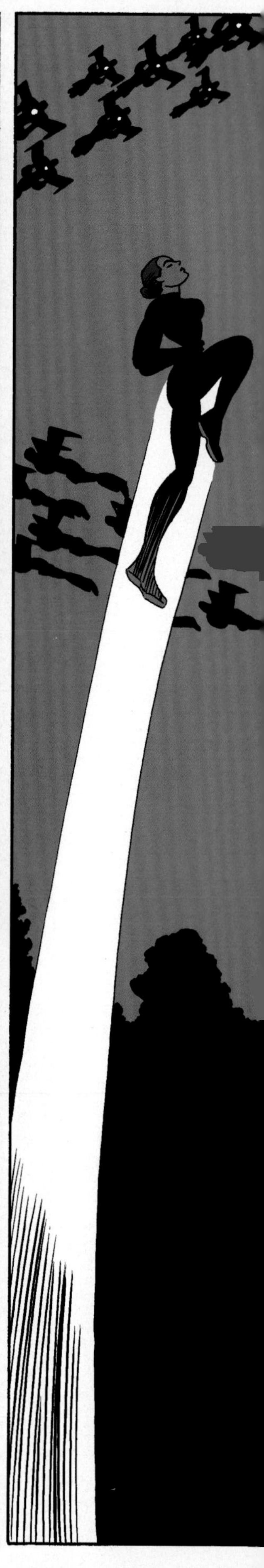

WE ARE UNDER ATTACK!
DESTROY HER!
ALL GLORY TO DOO--=KZKK=
KRUNK
GUESS YOU BETTER HIT THE ALARM, YEAH? CALL FOR REINFORCEMENTS?
EVEN I, THE LEAST OF LORD DOOM'S SERVANTS, NEEDS NO HELP TO DEAL WITH THE LIKES OF YOU.
ARE YOU SURE? I MEAN, YOUR BUDDY HERE DIDN'T DO THAT WELL. AND NOW YOU'RE ALONE. YOU SURE YOU DON'T WANT TO HIT THE ALARM?
YES, I AM SURE!

GAH. NOTHING'S SIMPLE.

OKAY, OKAY...

NOPE.

HMMM...
NOPE.

O...KAY.

BRAKOOMM
BOOM
BOOM
BOO
WOO!
ACK!

HEY!
TINY GREEN WOMAN, YOU HAVE BEGUN TO IRRITATE DOOM.
I TOLD YOU I'D COME FOR HIM.
I LAUGHED THEN, AND I LAUGH NOW.
WHY HAVE YOU COME HERE, SMALL WOMAN? DO YOU CARE FOR MY SON SO MUCH? DO YOU LOVE HIM? YOU WOULD NOT BE THE FIR--

DO YOU?

YOU DARE?

SURE DO.

CRASH
I DIDN'T COME HERE TO RESCUE KRISTOFF. I CAME FOR YOU, DOOM. WE NEED TO TALK. ABOUT YOUR SON.
I DON'T THINK HE REALLY WANTS TO LEAVE LATVERIA. HE JUST WANTS A CHANCE TO BE HIS OWN PERSON.
BUT YOU'VE GOT HIM SO BEATEN DOWN, SO CONTROLLED, THAT HE DOESN'T KNOW WHO THAT IS.
YOU AREN'T TURNING HIM INTO A RULER, DOOM. YOU'RE RAISING SOMEONE WHO ONLY KNOWS HOW TO BOW.

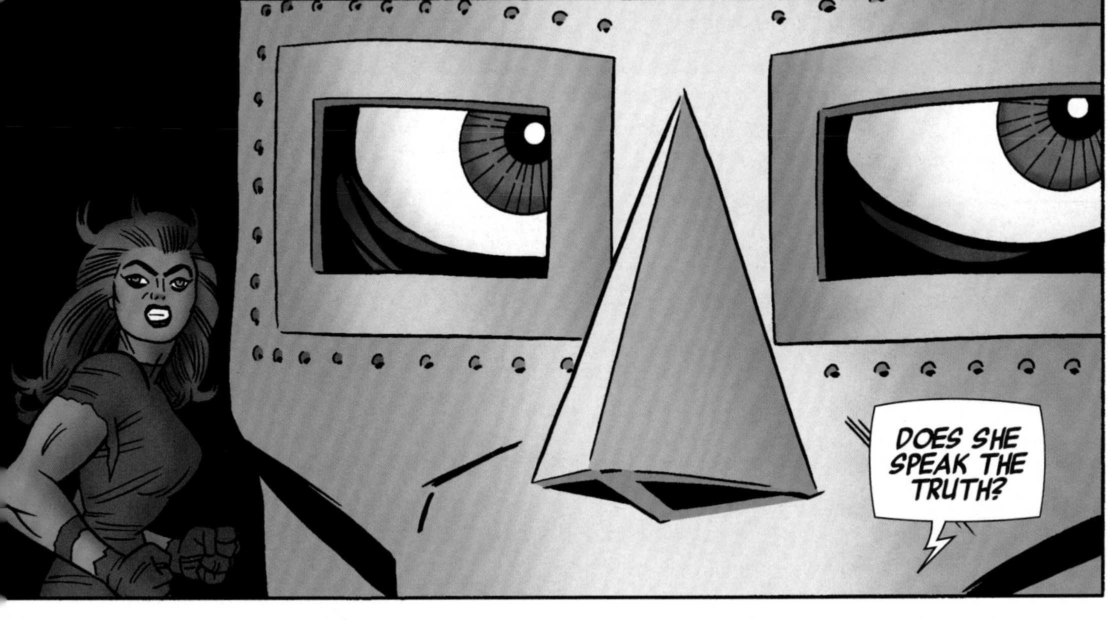
DOES SHE SPEAK THE TRUTH?

THANK YOU FOR COMING, MS. WALTERS. I APPRECIATE IT.
WELL. YEAH. YOU'RE A CLIENT.
ANSWER DOOM! YOUR PATHETIC ATTEMPT TO DEFECT WAS NOT SIMPLY ANOTHER PLEA FOR ATTENTION?
YOU WOULD RATHER GIVE UP THE THRONE THAN RULE AS I INSTRUCT?
YES, FATHER. I SHOULD HAVE DONE THIS LONG AGO.
YOU WOULD NOT ALLOW YOUR LIFE TO BE DICTATED IN EVERY RESPECT BY ANOTHER.
WHY SHOULD YOU EXPECT ANY LESS FROM YOUR SON?
SO. I DO NOT WISH TO LEAVE. BUT I MUST HAVE A LIFE. IF I CANNOT HAVE IT HERE, I WILL HAVE IT ELSEWHERE.

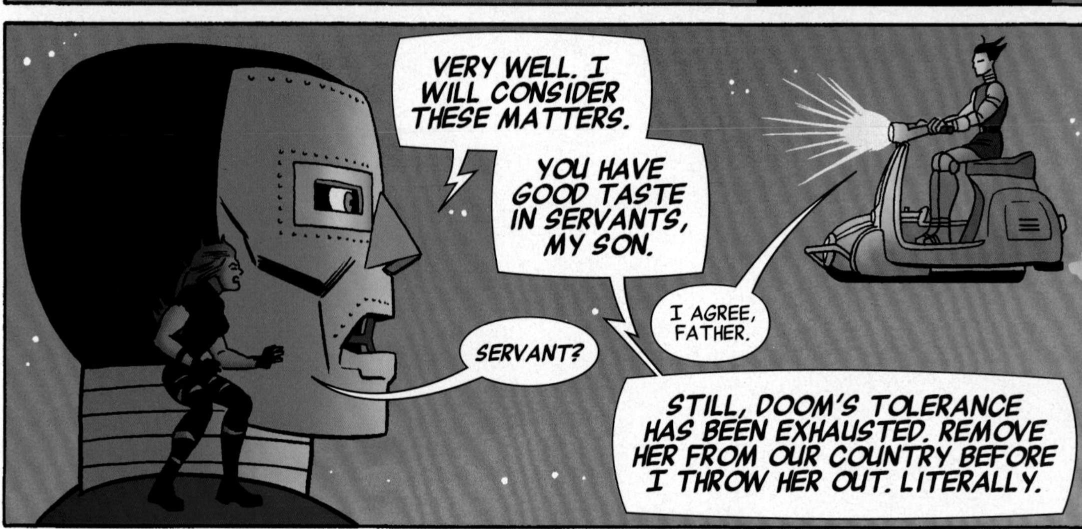
VERY WELL. I WILL CONSIDER THESE MATTERS.
YOU HAVE GOOD TASTE IN SERVANTS, MY SON.
I AGREE, FATHER.
SERVANT?
STILL, DOOM'S TOLERANCE HAS BEEN EXHAUSTED. REMOVE HER FROM OUR COUNTRY BEFORE I THROW HER OUT. LITERALLY.

READY?
KIND OF WANT TO WRECK THIS GIGANTIC DOOM, BUT...
DO NOT WRECK THIS GIGANTIC DOOM.
YEAH. READY.

THANK YOU. YOU ARE A GOOD SERVANT.
I AM NOT A--
I KNOW.
HILARIOUS.
I DO APPRECIATE EVERYTHING YOU'VE DONE FOR ME, THOUGH. PLEASE--SEND ME AN INVOICE FOR YOUR SERVICES. I WILL SEE THAT IT IS PAID IMMEDIATELY ON RECEIPT.
ANY CHANCE YOU COULD PAY WITH SOMETHING BESIDES LATVERIAN FRANCS?
...
NO.
FABULOUS.

BACK IN BROOKLYN. LAW OFFICES OF JENNIFER WALTERS, PLLC
HI, PATSY. THANK YOU FOR COMING IN.
NO PROBLEM, JEN. YOU ALWAYS HAVE INTERESTING STUFF GOING ON. MORE THAN I DO, ANYWAY.
BESIDES, IT'S MY JOB, RIGHT? ACTUALLY, WE SHOULD TALK ABOUT THAT. YOU ARE GOING TO PAY ME, RIGHT?
OF COURSE, PATSY--WE JUST HAD A TRICKY SITUATION WITH OUR LAST ROUND OF BILLING, AND--
I ALMOST WENT TO JAIL FOR TRAFFICKING IN ILLEGAL CURRENCY!
INC
ER...
OKAY, LET'S TRY TO FOCUS. THE REASON FOR THIS MEETING IS--

OH, HEY, SORRY, DIDN'T REALIZE ANYONE HAD THE ROOM. YOU GUYS GONNA BE LONG?
COME ON.
HI, RUFUS. WE'VE JUST GOT IT FOR THE HOUR.

GREAT. JUST NEED SOMEPLACE TO TEST THIS THING. REZA WOULDN'T LET ME TURN IT ON IN THE LAB. SAID IT WAS TOO DANGEROUS.
PFFT.
WHERE'S THE TRUST, YOU KNOW?

ZZXH

HUH.

ROOM'S ALL YOURS, GUYS!

WHO WAS THAT?
RUFUS RANDALL. HE'S... AN INVENTOR, I GUESS. THIS BUILDING'S FULL OF GUYS LIKE THAT.
THINGS BLOW UP AROUND HERE ALL THE TIME. I HAVE TO WEAR HEADPHONES TO GET ANYTHING DONE.
RU...FUS... RAN...DALL. HMMM.
AN...Y...WAY!
SOME TIME BACK, I WAS RESEARCHING A CASE. I FOUND THIS.
FILED
IT'S A MOTION TO CHANGE VENUE IN A CASE IN NORTH DAKOTA. IT WAS MISFILED, BURIED IN A BOX ABOUT SOMETHING TOTALLY UNRELATED.
THIS...IS THE BLUE FILE. FOR THE MOMENT, IT IS OUR ONE ACTIVE CASE.
I'VE BEEN TRYING TO AVOID DEALING WITH IT, BUT UNTIL WE GET MORE CLIENTS, IT'S EITHER THIS OR WE SIT AROUND WAITING FOR THE PHONE TO RING.
THE PROBLEM IS, THE BLUE FILE MAKES NO SENSE.
MS. WALTERS, THIS NAMES YOU AS A DEFENDANT.
AND A LOT OF OTHER PEOPLE WE KNOW--WYATT WINGFOOT...GREER GRANT NELSON...THAT'S TIGRA. AND ISN'T HERMAN SCHULTZ SHOCKER?
DO YOU KNOW THE SUBSTANCE OF THE CLAIM? THE REASON THIS...GEORGE SAYWITZ WAS SUING ALL OF YOU?
AS I SAID, IT MAKES NO SENSE. BUT I'M HOPING YOU TWO CAN HELP ME.
NO. THAT'S THE PROBLEM. I DON'T REMEMBER THIS AT ALL. I HAVE NO IDEA WHAT THIS IS ABOUT.
THEY WOULDN'T HAVE MOVED TO CHANGE VENUE UNLESS YOU'D ALL BEEN PROPERLY SERVED. YOU MUST HAVE BEEN NOTIFIED--RECEIVED A COPY OF THE COMPLAINT, AT LEAST.
I AM AWARE OF THAT, ANGIE, BUT NO. NOTHING. THE FILE NUMBER COMES UP EMPTY IN NORTH DAKOTA'S RECORDS.
ANGIE, YOU'RE ON RESEARCH. REALLY DIG DEEP ON THIS. CALL THE CLERKS IN NORTH DAKOTA, SWEET-TALK THEM A LITTLE, SEE WHAT YOU CAN FIND.
PATSY, YOU'RE MY INVESTIGATOR--IT'S TIME FOR YOU TO INVESTIGATE. INTERVIEW AS MANY OF THESE DEFENDANTS AS YOU CAN. SEE IF ANY OF THEM KNOWS ANYTHING ABOUT THIS.
MAYBE IT'S JUST A FILING ERROR, BUT IT DOESN'T FEEL LIKE ONE. THIS FEELS...

...IMPORTANT.
NEXT:
BLUE

CAPTAIN MARVEL #4

When former U.S. Air Force pilot Carol Danvers was caught in the explosion of an alien device called the Psyche-Magnitron, she was transformed into one of the world's most powerful super beings. She now uses her abilities to protect her planet and fight for justice as an Avenger.
She is Earth's Mightiest Hero...she is...

CAPTAIN MARVEL

PREVIOUSLY

After the Builders destroyed her world, a young extraterrestrial girl named Tic was relocated with her people to the planet Torfa, a poison planet that is slowly killing the refugees living on it. Tic travelled to Earth to seek help and returned with Captain Marvel, inadvertently putting Earth's Mightiest Hero in the middle of an intergalactic turf war.

HIGHER, FURTHER, FASTER, MORE. PART FOUR

KELLY SUE DeCONNICK — WRITER
DAVID LOPEZ — ART
LEE LOUGHRIDGE — COLOR ART
VC'S JOE CARAMAGNA — LETTERER
DAVID LOPEZ — COVER ARTIST
DEVIN LEWIS — ASSISTANT EDITOR
SANA AMANAT — EDITOR
NICK LOWE — SENIOR EDITOR
AXEL ALONSO — EDITOR IN CHIEF
JOE QUESADA — CHIEF CREATIVE OFFICER
DAN BUCKLEY — PUBLISHER
ALAN FINE — EXEC. PRODUCER

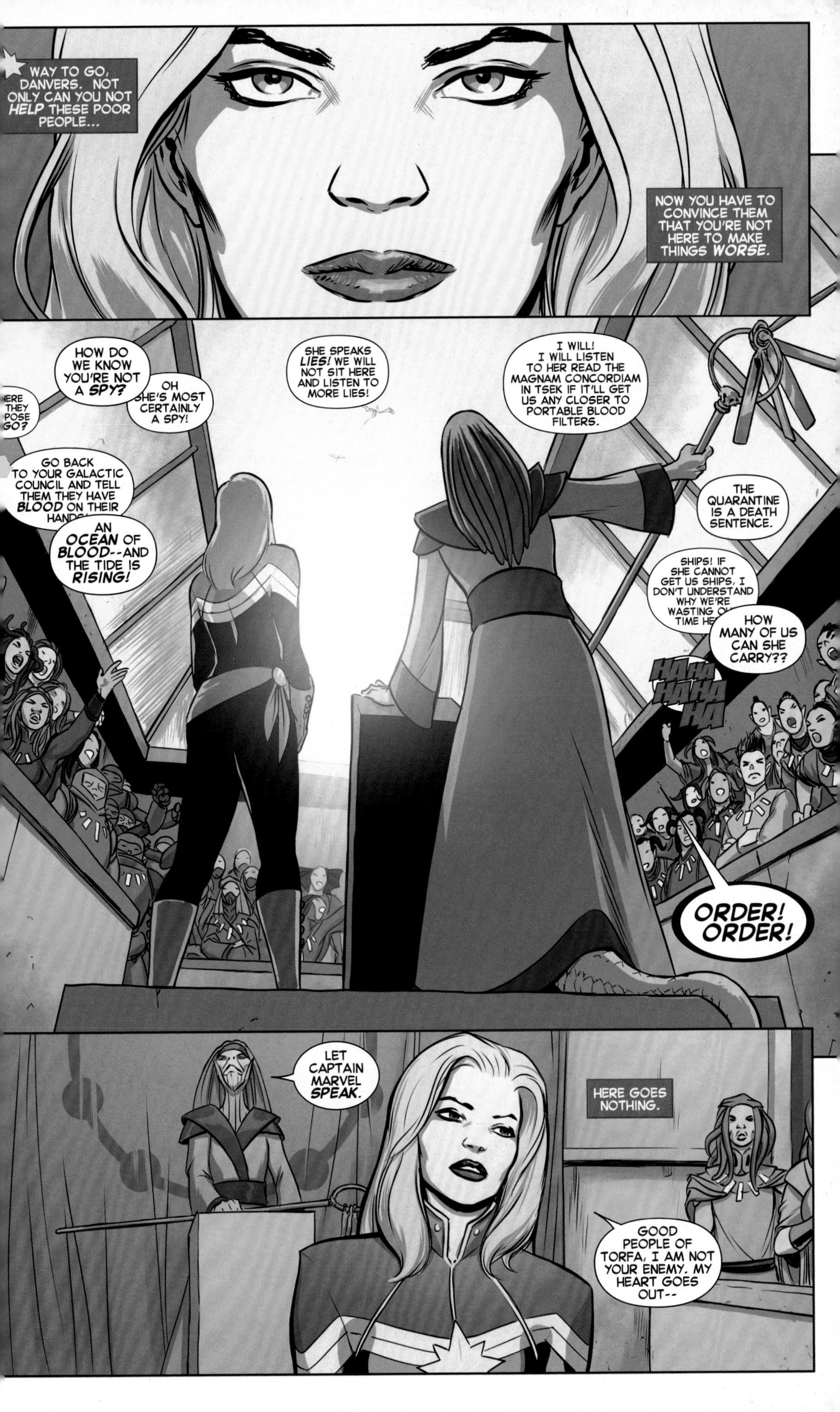
WAY TO GO, DANVERS. NOT ONLY CAN YOU NOT HELP THESE POOR PEOPLE...
NOW YOU HAVE TO CONVINCE THEM THAT YOU'RE NOT HERE TO MAKE THINGS WORSE.
HOW DO WE KNOW YOU'RE NOT A SPY?
OH SHE'S MOST CERTAINLY A SPY!
SHE SPEAKS LIES! WE WILL NOT SIT HERE AND LISTEN TO MORE LIES!
I WILL! I WILL LISTEN TO HER READ THE MAGNAM CONCORDIAM IN TSEK IF IT'LL GET US ANY CLOSER TO PORTABLE BLOOD FILTERS.
GO BACK TO YOUR GALACTIC COUNCIL AND TELL THEM THEY HAVE BLOOD ON THEIR HANDS!
AN OCEAN OF BLOOD--AND THE TIDE IS RISING!
THE QUARANTINE IS A DEATH SENTENCE.
SHIPS! IF SHE CANNOT GET US SHIPS, I DON'T UNDERSTAND WHY WE'RE WASTING OUR TIME HERE
HOW MANY OF US CAN SHE CARRY??
HA HA HA HA HA
ORDER! ORDER!
LET CAPTAIN MARVEL SPEAK.
HERE GOES NOTHING.
GOOD PEOPLE OF TORFA, I AM NOT YOUR ENEMY. MY HEART GOES OUT--

HER HEART?
WHAT WILL WE DO WITH YOUR HEART?
CAN WE TRADE IT FOR A SHIP?!
HA HA HA HA HA

ORDER!
THE CHAIR RECOGNIZES SONARA EK OF THE ARGEN.
MADAME ELEANIDES?

FORGIVE OUR GALLOWS HUMOR, CAPTAIN. FOR EVERY ONE YOU SEE HERE, THERE WERE A MILLION DEATHS WHEN THE BUILDERS DESTROYED OUR WORLDS.
I CAN'T PRETEND TO KNOW WHAT THAT MUST BE LIKE.

WE FEEL IT. WE FEEL THE WEIGHT OF A MILLION SOULS WITH EVERY STEP WE TAKE.

BUT FRIENDS, WHEN OUR PEOPLES WERE UNDER ATTACK ON THE RING WORLD, WAS IT NOT THE AVENGERS WHO DEFENDED THE HEAVENS SO WE COULD MAKE OUR ESCAPE?
IS IT SO HARD TO BELIEVE THAT THE GODS WOULD DELIVER TO US ONCE AGAIN--
OH, FOR LOVE OF--ARE YOU KIDDING ME?!

WITH ALL DUE RESPECT, SONARA, YOUR GODS HAVE NO PLACE IN THESE PROCEEDINGS!
NOR-- FRANKLY-- DOES THE AVENGER!

I MEAN NO OFFENSE.
NONE TAKEN.
MADAME ELEANIDES, IF I MAY?
MR. CEPUL OF THE SENTIMAULT HAS THE FLOOR.

FRIENDS...
THERE IS A SIMPLE SOLUTION TO OUR PLIGHT.

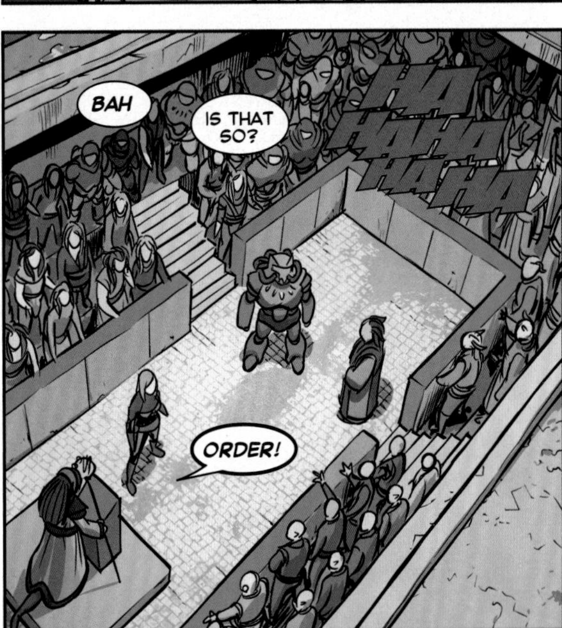
BAH
IS THAT SO?
HA HAHA HAHA
ORDER!

PLEASE, MR. CEPUL. ENLIGHTEN US.

LEAVE US. LEAVE THE SENTIMAULT TO LOOK AFTER YOUR ILL.

THERE ISN'T ANOTHER PLANET LIKE OUR HOME WORLD IN THE GALAXY. WE ARE NOT ADAPTABLE TO LIFE *HERE* OR ANYWHERE ELSE!
WE WILL NOT GIVE UP ON YOU, CEPUL. NOR WILL WE ALLOW YOU TO GIVE UP ON YOURSELVES.
NO!
NO! NO! NO!
NEVER AGAIN WILL WE PART!
ORDER! ORDER!
I BEG YOU: TAKE WHAT TRANSPORT THE ALLIANCE OFFERS YOU AND *SAVE YOURSELVES.* THE SENTIMAULT ARE DOOMED ANYWAY...
LET US STAY AND OFFER PALLIATIVE CARE TO YOUR--
NO! WE WILL NOT LEAVE THEM! *NOR YOU!* WE WILL *NOT!*
THE *ALLIANCE* OFFERS TO "EXTRACT US" BUT THEY CANNOT SAY TO *WHERE.* WE WOULD LIVE ON THE EVACUATION SHIPS FOR *WHO KNOWS* HOW LONG! THEY WOULD BECOME OUR PRISONS!
BETTER TO *LIVE* IN A PRISON, THAN *DIE* IN THE OPEN AIR.
THEN YOU HAVE NEVER BEEN TO PRISON.
I *AM* IN PRISON, *SONARA! LOOK AT ME!*
EXCUSE ME! EXCUSE ME!
EXCUSE ME!
THE AVENGER HAS THE FLOOR!

IF YOU HAD ADEQUATE TRANSPORT, COULD YOU TAKE THE AFFLICTED WITH YOU? IF YOU COULD ALL GO?
TAKE THEM WHERE?
ONE PROBLEM AT A TIME.
NO. THE ALLIANCE WON'T ACCEPT THEM FOR FEAR OF CONTAGION.

IF YOU HAD YOUR OWN SHIPS?
BUT WE DON'T.
NOT TRANSPORT, I KNOW, BUT YOU HAVE A FEW FIGHTERS. WHAT IF WE TRIED TO ENGINEER A FERRY RIG?
IF WE COULD GET ENOUGH THRUST TO REACH ORBIT, COULD WE BUILD ANOTHER RING WORLD?

NO.

AT LEAST I GOT THEM TO AGREE ON SOMETHING. WHY CAN'T ANYTHING EVER BE EASY?
WHY NOT?

GIL, SHOW THE GOOD CAPTAIN OUR "FLEET."
YES, MA'AM.

TA-DA.
THIS ISN'T A FLEET, THIS IS A JUNKYARD.
SURE AM GLAD YOU CAME HALFWAY ACROSS THE GALAXY TO TELL US THAT WE WERE DOOMED.
YOU WORK FOR THE GALACTIC ALLI--
I GET WHY YOU'RE HELLBENT ON MAKING ME YOUR ENEMY, BUT IT'S A WASTE OF YOUR TIME.
I DON'T "WORK FOR" ANYBODY!
I'M AN AVENGER. IN THE WAR WITH THE BUILDERS I FOUGHT ON THE SIDE OF THE ALLIANCE--AND SO DID YOU.
NOW THINGS ARE COMPLICATE PEOPLE ARE DYING. YOU WAN TO HIT SOMETHING AND YOU CAN'T PUNCH A DISEASE.
I GET IT. AND IF YOU WANT TO TAKE ANOTHER SWING AT ME, BIG GUY, WE WILL GO. RIGHT HERE, RIGHT NOW...
BUT IT'S NOT GOING TO MAKE YOU FEEL ANY LESS DOOMED.
SOMEBODY SAY DOOMED?

I'M SENTIMAULT. WE *LOVE* A GOOD GAME OF "WHO'S MORE DOOMED?"
B-329. FOLKS CALL ME "BEE."
OR "B-BOP"!

NO ONE CALLS YOU A "B-BOP."
FIRST, IT'S JUST "B-BOP" NOT "A B-BOP." "A B-BOP" IS NOT COOL. "B-BOP" IS COOL.
AND SECOND, NO ONE CALLS ME "B-BOP" *YET*.

EVERYTHING ALL RIGHT HERE?
EVERYTHING'S FINE. MR. GIL HERE AND I WERE JUST BONDING.

GRR!

THE FELLOWSHIP CALLED A RECESS. ALLIANCE WANTS A MEET WITH ELEANIDES AND SHE WISHES TO WAIT FOR THE REPORT ON YOUR IDEA.
THIS JUST IN: HER IDEA SUCKS.
NO, GIL, IT DOESN'T...

HER IDEA IS SOLID...
HER ABILITY...
...TO CARRY IT OUT...
...IS ALL THAT'S LACKING.

JA KYEE LRURT. WARLORD. GODDESS. YOU CALL ME "JACKIE."
EVER HELD THE HAND OF A GODDESS BEFORE?
YOU'RE NOT MY FIRST, ACTUALLY.
THAT DOESN'T SURPRISE ME ONE BIT.

"WARLORD" AND "GODDESS" ARE NOT EXACT TRANSLATIONS. JACKIE IS OUR CHIEF ENGINEER AND DEFENSE MINISTER.
I PREFER "WARLORD" AND "GODDESS."

SURE. WHO WOULDN'T?
KNEW YOU'D UNDERSTAND.
THE FELLOWSHIP INQUIRED ABOUT YOUR IDEA--BUILDING ORBITING RESIDENTIAL STATIONS AND USING THE FLEET TO TOW THEM OUT.

BEST IDEA I'VE HEARD. WE JUST DON'T HAVE THE RESOURCES. THESE THREE ARE THE CLOSEST I'VE GOT TO COMBAT-READY AND BETWEEN THEM THEY'RE NOT--
WHAT ABOUT THE THE ROCKET RIG?
OH, YOU MEAN THE ROCKET RIG THAT SOMEBODY TOOK TO ***EARTH*** AND NEGLECTED TO ***RETURN?***
I MEANT THE ROCKET RIG THAT ***SOMEBODY*** SAID WOULD NEVER MAKE IT TO ***ORBIT***, LET ALONE ***EARTH***.
I DIDN'T ***ASK--***
SETTLE, GIRL. YOU'RE LUCKY JACKIE FORGIVES.
THE ROCKET RIG
S NO HELP ANYWAY.
SSUMING WE EVEN
HAD SOMETHING
TO TOW--
BRMMBBLLL
HAFFENSYEEEEEEEEE!
WHAT'S HAPPENING? WHAT IS THAT?

GRRRRRR!
I HAD A RUN-IN WITH THE HAFF ON THE WAY INTO TORFA--WHAT'S THEIR INTEREST HERE?
VRUUSH
THEY'RE PIRATES, THIEVES AND SMUGGLERS. THEY'VE GOT AN INTEREST ANYWHERE THERE'S SOMETHING TO STEAL AND NO ONE TO STOP THEM!

I'M GOING--
NO, DON'T!
YOU'LL NEVER CATCH THEM WITHOUT A SHIP.

HURGH!
VRUSH

ALLIANCE PULLED THEIR PATROLS, SO HAFFENSYE COME AND GO AS THEY PLEASE. TRADE SHIPS CAN'T GET THROUGH.

THE ALLIANCE IS STARVING US OUT AND THE HAFF ARE SPEEDING UP THE PROCESS.

AND BECAUSE I CAN'T GET PARTS--
JACKIE--
I CAN'T GET A PATROL IN THE AIR TO STOP THEM!
JACKIE--!

HH
NO ONE
O STOP
EM," LIKE
HELL!
CHKA
CHKA CHKA
EENSYYYYYYYYYYYEEEE!
THE HAFFENSYE ARE AN INTERGALACTIC CRIMINAL NETWORK. WITH ALL DUE RESPECT, YOU'VE BARELY BEEN ON THIS PLANET TEN MINUTES. WHAT COULD YOU HAVE THAT THEY'D WANT?
IT'S NOT WHAT THEY WANT. IT'S WHAT THEY DON'T WANT US TO HAVE.
FOOD. MEDICINE. WHO KNOWS WHAT ALL ELSE.
MAYBE YOU COULD PHONE 'EM UP AND ASK 'EM.
WE CAN USE MY SHIP. WE CAN GO AFTER THEM.
RIGHT NOW.
!

STRAP IN.
TOO LATE TO PICK UP ON THEIR HEAT SIGNATURE. SO WHERE AM I MOST LIKELY TO RUN INTO HAFFENSYE?
URSOR 2 OR URSOR 4. NO NATURAL RESOURCES, NO OVERSIGHT. IF YOU CAN'T BUY IT ON UR2 OR UR4, IT CAN'T BE BOUGHT.
HARRISON, LAY IN A COURSE FOR URSOR 2.
AYE, CAPTAIN.
C'MON, BEE! WHAT'S THE MATTER?
ISN'T THIS WHAT WE WERE...
...HOPING FOR.

"MADAME," IS IT? PRESIDENT? KING? QUEEN? WHAT HAVE YOU DECIDED ON?
"MADAME" IS FINE, EMPEROR J'SON.
YOU'RE A TERRIBLE LIAR, MADAME ELEANIDES.
YOU DON'T HAVE HE BALLS TO MAKE THE HARD CALLS, AFTER ALL.
I BEG YOUR PARDON...?
YOU WILL, MADAME, SOONER OR LATER.
IF YOU MEAN TO RENDER MEDICAL AID, YOU ARE MOST WELCOME.
BUT IF THE COUNCIL SENT THE SPARTAX EMPEROR HIMSELF TO THREATEN--
THE GALACTIC COUNCIL DOES NOT SEND AN EMPEROR ON DISPATCH!
I AM NOT AN ERRAND BOY! THIS IS MY TERRITORY. THERE IS NO HIGHER AUTHORITY. I AM NOT JUST YOUR LEADER, WOMAN, I AM YOUR GOD!
...
THEN I PRAY YOU...
...HAVE MERCY ON US.

REMEMBERED WHO WE ARE! FOUND THE WILL TO LIVE AGAIN!
LIBERATED A BUNCH OF ENGINE PARTS!
WHY ARE YOU RUNNING?
WE'RE BEING CHASED!
YOU FOUND THE HAFFENSYE?
NO...BUT WE FOUND THEIR BUYERS!

YOU STOLE THOSE PARTS!
THEY STOLE THEM FIRST.

WELL...

THAT'S DIFFERENT.
I LIKE YOU SO MUCH ALREADY.
CUT THE CHITCHAT, JACKIE--GET ON THE SHIP!
SEE? IT'S LIKE YOU'VE KNOWN ME ALL MY LIFE.
HARRISON, LIFT OFF! I'LL CATCH UP!
ROGER, CAPTAIN.
SPARTAX...!
WHAT ARE THE ROYAL GUARD DOING HERE?
J'SON...

YOU SAID I WOULD BEG, MY LIEGE, AND HERE I AM.
HOW CLEVER AND POWERFUL YOU MUST FEEL.
THREE DAYS, ELEANIDES. YOU HAVE THREE DAYS TO ORGANIZE AN EVACUATION. WE CAN TRANSPORT ONE THOUSAND OF YOUR YOUNGEST AND HEALTHIEST AND RESETTLE THEM. THE REST...
THE REST WILL DIE.

THE REST WILL DIE EITHER WAY!
WOULD YOU PREFER TO ALL DIE?!

IS THAT SO HARD TO UNDERSTAND?
WE HAVE, EACH OF US, ALREADY LOST ONE PLANET, ONE PEOPLE. YES, WE WOULD RATHER FIGHT THIS PLAGUE AND DIE TOGETHER THAN SUFFER THAT FATE AGAIN!

HAVE MERCY. I BEG YOU.

THIS IS MY MERCY.

IN THREE DAYS WE WILL COME. IN THREE DAYS YOU WILL LEAVE THIS ROCK, OR YOU WILL GET YOUR WISH--
THIS IS MADNESS--

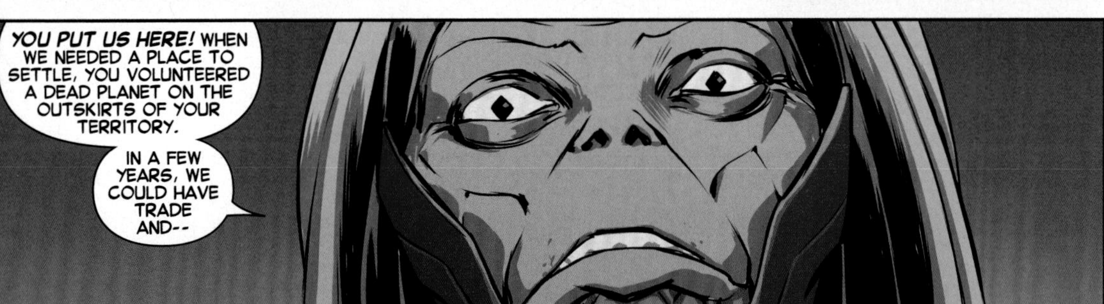
YOU PUT US HERE! WHEN WE NEEDED A PLACE TO SETTLE, YOU VOLUNTEERED A DEAD PLANET ON THE OUTSKIRTS OF YOUR TERRITORY.
IN A FEW YEARS, WE COULD HAVE TRADE AND--

YES! I PUT YOU HERE! AND THEN YOUR PEOPLE BEGAN TO FALL ILL AND DIE AND YOU WERE UNABLE TO MAKE THE TOUGH CALLS AND SO NOW I MUST!
HEAVY IS THE HEAD THAT WEARS THE CROWN, MADAME.

THREE DAYS.
YOU WILL LEAVE THIS PLACE OR THE SPARTAX FORCES WILL SET UPON YOU LIKE TIRGENS ON FOOM AND YOU WILL ALL DIE HERE TOGETHER!
WHY? WHY--?
BECAUSE IT IS MY WILL!

HARRISON, SET EVASIVE COURSE FOR...?
MANIACIANO OUTPOST, URSOR 4.
YOU HEARD THE LADY.
SETTING EVASIVE COURSE.
AWWW, LOOKIE, LOOKIE, LOOKIE WHAT WE GOT HERE!
WHAT'S IT DO?
WE COULD CAST A MOLD OFF OF THIS ONE AND MAKE A FEW MORE...
IF WE HAD MATERIALS, MAYBE.
I GOT A FEW SPARE PARTS.
EW! HUH-- UH. I AM NOT GOING TO FLY A SHIP MADE OUT OF YOUR SPARE PARTS-- NO SIR!
THEY'RE NOT SPARE SPARE, REALLY. I JUST DON'T USE 'EM THAT MUCH.
IS ONE OF 'EM YOUR HEAD?
OH, THAT WAS GOOD. ARE YOU PROUD OF THAT ONE, GIL?
I AM A LITTLE BIT, YEAH.
HARRISON! PLAY SOMETHING A GAL CAN DANCE TO!
YES, JACKIE.

YOU KNOW THE SPARTAX EMPEROR.
A BIT.

HE WAS THE ONE WHO TRIED TO CUT A DEAL WITH THE BUILDERS AND LED THEM TO THE RING WORLD.

I REMEMBER. I WAS THERE.

THEN YOU KNOW HE CAN'T BE TRUSTED.
I KNOW HE WAS TRYING TO *SAVE* HIS PEOPLE.

WHAT WERE HIS SECRET POLICE DOING ON URSOR 2?
LOOKING TO BUY SOMETHING SKETCHY, IF I HAD TO GUESS.
WHATEVER THEY WERE AFTER... THINK WE CAN FIND IT FIRST?

YOU, ME AND THOSE FREAKS BACK THERE...?
I WOULD'T BET AGAINST US, TIC.

MANIACIANO OUTPOST.
URSOR 4.
"OKAY. LET'S TRY THIS AGAIN."
SAME PLAN AS THE LAST STOP EXCEPT, TIC, YOU STAY WITH ME.
BEE, JACKIE, GIL--SPLIT UP. IF YOU THINK YOU'VE GOT A LEGIT SOURCE, SIGNAL AND I'LL MAKE THE BUY.
AYE, CAPTAIN MARVEL.
EASY-PEASY, IN AND OUT.
...WHAT COULD POSSIBLY GO WRONG?
TO BE CONTINUED

MS. MARVEL #4

Hey! Lady! Wake up! Please--
SO, I'M PRETTY SURE I JUST GOT SHOT.
I didn't mean to! It just--went off!
Whose fault is that, moron?
Hers! She was squeezing me so hard I thought I was gonna puke!
I WANT TO SIT UP-- I WANT TO SAY SOMETHING--BUT MY MOUTH WON'T OPEN AND MY BODY WON'T MOVE.
I gotta call the cops-- she needs an ambulance--
No! Don't! I'm so dead if you do!
NO AMBULANCE-- BRUNO, DON'T CALL AN AMBULANCE--
I should let the cops pick you up. It'd serve you right.
You wouldn't do that. Our nonna would die of shame. Come on, Bruno--
Get out of here. Go!

Yeah, hello? I need an ambulance at 357 West Side Avenue.
Ms. Marvel just got shot in my store.
ASIAN WEDDING LEFTOVERS
N-no--
Huh?
They can't--see me--I'm not Ms. Marvel--
Sorry, Captain Marvel. Help is coming. Don't try to move--
Bruno-- it's me--
Yeah, I know. I saw you yesterday on the news.
No-- listen--
--it's me.
ADOBO FILIPINO TAKE OUT
TORPEDOES HALF PRICE

--it's Kamala.

ARVEL COMICS
ROUDLY PRESENTS:
PAST CURFEW
PART FOUR OF FIVE
Kamala Khan has always felt different.
Strict parents, nerdy hobbies and now... strange shape-shifting powers?
But maybe this is good! Maybe Kamala can do great things like saving Bruno from a robbery at the Circle Q posing as the original Ms. Marvel!
Except... getting SHOT isn't so great.
BLAM!
WILLOW WILSON - writer
ADRIAN ALPHONA - art
IAN HERRING - color art
VC'S JOE CARAMAGNA - lettering
MIE MCKELVIE & MATT WILSON - cover art
EVIN LEWIS - asst editor
SANA AMANAT - editor
ICK LOWE - senior editor
AXEL ALONSO - editor in chief
OE QUESADA - chief creative officer
AN BUCKLEY - publisher
LAN FINE - executive producer

I--I don't understand.
I have to hide. The police--they can't know it's me.
My parents will freak, the NSA will wiretap our mosque or something, and then they'll sell me to science!
Okay. Okay. I don't--
Leaving aside the fact that you somehow got super-powers and didn't tell me, your second-best friend, you need immediate medical attention.
No, I don't! I'm--
--fine?
I--I healed.
As soon as I went back to my regular self, I healed. This is amazing.
This is weird.

Where's the bullet?
It may have fallen down the back of my pants.
What is going on? What is happening? I cannot process this.
Imagine how I feel. I've been obsessively searching the Internet all weekend, trying to figure out if I have some kind of disease.
Ta-da!
ASIAN WEDDING LEFTOVERS
Hold on, hold on--does this mean you saved Zoe after the party the other night? That was your picture all over the news?!

I can't believe you didn't tell me about any of this!
I'm sorry, Bruno. I wanted to, but--
I was so mad at you for ratting me out to my parents, and this whole powers thing hasn't exactly been easy.
But why hide? You saved Zoe, you just saved the Circle Q-- why do it all behind someone else's face?
At first, I couldn't control the shape-shifting. And then--it just made sense to keep going.
After that thing on the news, everybody's expecting Ms. Marvel. A real super hero. With perfect hair and big boots. Not Kamala Khan from Jersey City.
Who cares what people expect? Maybe they expect some perfect blonde, what I need-- I mean, what we need-- is you.
You're the coolest girl I've ever met. You say what you mean and you kick butt at video games and you're smart and funny and--
...
You can keep saying stuff.
Nah, I think I'm done.
CIRCLE
AMBULANCE

They can't see me like this!
Ggh--
What's going on? Are you okay?
Not done healing, apparently.
I'm not clear on the rules, but I guess I can't heal when I'm shape-shifting or something.
Dramatic irony, bruh!
Here! Put this on!
Am I hiding my identity or taking a nap?
Poke eyeholes in it!

Jersey City police!
Where's Ms. Marvel?
Here. I'm Ms. Marvel.
This supposed to be a prank or something, kid? Cause you don't look like Ms. Marvel to me.
What's Ms. Marvel supposed to look like?
You know. Tall, blonde, with the big... powers.
Oh. Okay. Well--
CRUNCH!
I've got big powers.

Great. Another one.
All right. All right. I believe you.
But we're responding to an armed robbery and possible gunshot fatality. So you'd better start explaining, or I'm hauling you kids in for making a false report.
There was a robbery. Or there would have been, except I squeezed he guy pretty good. That's when he shot me.
He idn't mean to.
"Didn't mean to." You knew this guy, then?
No. He was wearing a mask. He ran out after the gun went off.
Interesting.
Expect a subpoena for today's security tapes. I'll be keeping an eye on this place.
Costumed kids these days, I tell ya. My buddy in Brooklyn took a call once cause a guy was shooting arrows off his roof. Know who he was?
Hawkeye.
The guy who shot me...
It was Vick. Wasn't it? I recognized his voice.
Yeah. It was Vick.

I've gotta help him, Kamala. I'm his big brother. He's mixed up in something weird.
Weird how?
He was rambling about someone called the Inventor.
CLOSED
And how'd he get that gun? He's done some stupid stuff in his time, but now he's desperate. And scared. And I don't know why.
So let me help.
No way. It could be dangerous. I'll handle it.
I'm the one with super-powers.
What am I supposed to do with super-powers besides help my friends?
I don't know! Hold press conferences like that Tony Stark guy!
You protect me from stuff all the time. You have since we were kids.
But now I'm the stronger one, and I'm gonna protect you, and that totally freaks you out.
You're right.
It totally freaks me out.

I just don't want you to get *hurt*. You know?
I ***know***. But I put my foot in this mess--you guys were working it out, and I charged in to play the hero and made everything more ***complicated***.
I feel sort of ***responsible***.
CLOSED
Okay. Okay. I know how it goes when you decide you're gonna do something.
I'll tell you what I know if you ***promise*** to be careful.
I will.
But if I'm ***really*** going to do this--if I'm going to run around JC all ***powered up***--I'm gonna ***need*** something.
What?
ON TH' ADOBO
FILIPINO TAKE OUT
A ***costume***.
Obviously.
EATING UNDERWATER
THE JOY OF COOKING RARE ANIMALS
MOMJITSU
SUPERHERO PAPARAZZI
DROPKICK ENTHUSIAST

I'VE BEEN PLAYING VIDEO GAMES AND RPGs SINCE I WAS A LITTLE KID. I HAVE THE THUMBS TO PROVE IT.
KARACHI CHOP JONES
Ammi! Where's my burkini?
I READ A STUDY ONCE THAT SAID VIDEO GAMERS HAV THE REFLEXES OF FIGHTER PILOTS AN THE BODIES OF SEA SLUGS.
The one you said you would never wear?
I said I'd never wear it swimming. I didn't say I'd never wear it to, like, a party or something.
WITH THESE POWERS, I'VE CONVENIENTLY CIRCUMVENTED THE SEA SLUG THING.
IT'S TIME TO BREAK OUT THE GEEK FU.
You're grounded, remember? No parties.
I know. I'm not going to a party. I just... need this for...a project.

Hey!
NO. No "hey."
What project requires a burkini at 10 PM on a school night?
Obviously I'm gonna go party with my ten atheist boyfriends.
Really, Kamala? This sarcastic language to me? Is this the daughter I raised?
I'm warning you, beta. After I leave this room, I am locking the doors. And I am setting my alarm for 1 AM.
If I wake up and find you have snuck out again, the next step will involve Sheikh Abdullah.
What?! He hates me!
Then you'd better think very carefully about what you do next.
Good night.
OH MAN. NOW I'M ON THE CLOCK. THIS JUST KEEPS GETTING BETTER AND BETTER.
AMMI AND ABU TAUGHT ME TO ALWAYS THINK ABOUT THE GREATER GOOD. TO DEFEND PEOPLE WHO CAN'T DEFEND THEMSELVES, EVEN IF IT MEANS PUTTING YOURSELF AT RISK.
Bruno? I'm good to go.
Tell me where I'm heading.
I WISH THEY COULD SEE THAT THAT'S EXACTLY WHAT I'M TRYING TO DO.

"Vick's been hanging around an abandoned house out in Greenville. He doesn't know I know. I pulled the GPS data off his cell."
"You mean you opened up the Maps app and looked at the last place he'd been."
"Oh come on, dude. Let me feel like a secret agent for a minute.
"No drama, right, Kamala? You promised. Surveillance only."
"Right. Just peeking around."
I don't understand why we gotta keep watch. Everybody else is asleep.
Doyle's orders.
Know what I think?
What?
I think we're not supposed to be keeping other people out as much as keeping Vick in.
Doyle was really pissed about him messing up that robbery. Apparently Vick sai something. About the Inventor.
SPESHAL SODA

Dude, he's screwed.
Yup.
HEY!
WHAAAA!
UNGH!
Wh- who are you?!

WHO AM I? IT SEEMS LIKE AN EASY QUESTION. AND THEN I REALIZE...
MAYBE WHAT I SAID TO THOSE COPS WASN'T A JOKE. MAYBE THE NAME BELONGS TO WHOEVER HAS THE COURAGE TO FIGHT.
AND SO I TELL THEM.
You can call me Ms. Marvel.
And if you cooperate, I won't throw you again.
I TELL THEM WHO I AM.
Sit back to back with your hands together. Pretend we're on a cop show.
Where are you keeping Vick?
H-he's in the basement.
You don't want to go in there, trust me.
Why not?
There's stuff down there.
Yeah, and other kids who are less stupid than we are. Like Doyle.
You're making a big mistake!
THE BIRDMAN COMETH

Creepy.
Hunh?!!
Umph!
Just like a boss fight in World of Battlecraft... just like a boss fight in World of Battlecraft...
Nngh!

SCREEE!
Die, spooky robot thing!
Oh boy.
Ggh!
OWW!

SCREEEEE!
Get-- off!
THE BASEMENT-- I GOTTA GET TO THE BASEMENT--
SCREEE--
Huhh!
SLAM!

PROPERTY OF THE INVENTOR
Who is it? Who's there?

It's okay. It's me.
I mean--

FIGHT LOSER II
I'm Ms. Marvel.
I'm here to save you, Vittorio Carrelli.

PROPERTY OF THE INVENTOR
Oh really?
And how exactly do you plan to do that?
IMA BAD GUY
TO BE CONTINUED!

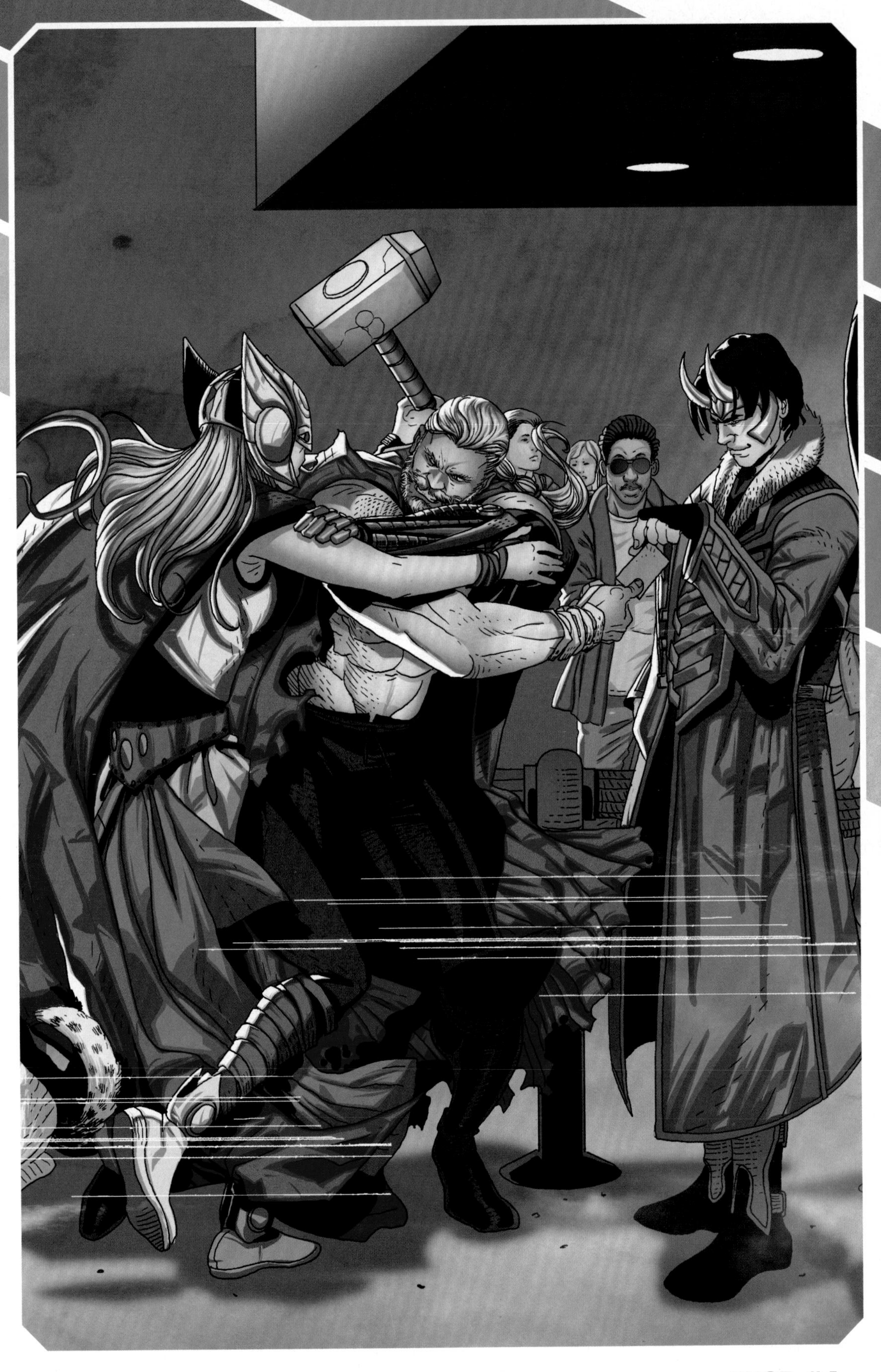

THOR #4

Welcome Home Variant by Salvador Larroca & Israel Silva

THOR #4

NEW THOR HAS RISEN.

TER THOR ODINSON FOUND HIMSELF NO LONGER WORTHY OF WIELDING MJOLNIR, A MYSTERIOUS OMAN WAS ABLE TO LIFT THE ENCHANTED HAMMER AND BECAME THE NEW GODDESS OF THUNDER.

ID JUST IN TIME, TOO. BECAUSE THE DARK ELF SORCERER MALEKITH HAS TEAMED UP WITH THE OST GIANTS OF JOTUNHEIM TO LAUNCH AN ASSAULT ON THE ROXXON ENERGY CORPORATION IN ARCH OF THE SKULL OF THE LAST GREAT KING OF JOTUNHEIM, LAUFEY.

ARIO AGGER, CEO OF ROXXON, WAS HIDING MORE THAN ANCIENT ARTIFACTS AND SHADY BUSINESS ALS—HE ALSO COULD TRANSFORM INTO A HALF-MAN, HALF-BULL BEAST—THE MONSTROUS INOTAUR OF LEGEND.

A DARK ELF, A MINOTAUR, AND THE NEW THOR WALK INTO A BAR. EXCEPT INSTEAD OF A BAR, IT'S A CRET VAULT CONTAINING THE SKULL OF A GIANT KING THAT HAS THE POWER TO PLUNGE THE TEN ALMS INTO WAR. WHAT COULD GO WRONG?

ELL, PLENTY. CHIEFLY: THE DISGRACED THOR ODINSON SHOWED UP TOO. AND HE *REALLY* WANTS IAT HAMMER BACK.

THOR VS. THOR

ASON AARON
WRITER

RUSSELL DAUTERMAN
ARTIST

MATTHEW WILSON
COLOR ARTIST

VC's JOE SABINO
LETTERER & PRODUCTION

RUSSELL DAUTERMAN & MATTHEW WILSON
COVER ARTISTS

SALVADOR LARROCA & ISRAEL SILVA
VARIANT COVER ARTISTS

JON MOISAN
ASSISTANT EDITOR

WIL MOSS
EDITOR

AXEL ALONSO
EDITOR IN CHIEF

JOE QUESADA
CHIEF CREATIVE OFFICER

DAN BUCKLEY
PUBLISHER

ALAN FINE
EXECUTIVE PRODUCER

THOR CREATED BY STAN LEE, LARRY LIEBER & JACK KIRBY

HOURS AGO. ASGARDIA. CITY OF THE GODS.
IN MY TIME, I HAVE KNOWN WAR AND HEL AND RAGNAROK.
I HAVE BLED ENOUGH TO FILL OCEANS.
I HAVE DIED.
FOR MORE YEARS THAN THERE ARE STARS, I HAVE WALKED THESE MANY REALMS, FACING HORRORS THAT COULD DRIVE EVEN A GOD TO UTTER MADNESS. BUT THIS...
WHERE IS IT?!
THIS MAY BE THE WORST WEEK OF MY LIFE.
WHERE THE HEL IS MY ARM?!?
IN THE BELLY OF A WHALE, MOST LIKE. AFTER YOUR FOOLISH LITTLE STUNT, YOU ARE LUCKY THERE IS ANYTHING LEFT OF YOU, BOY.
IF YOUR GOAT HADN'T DRAGGED YOU BACK HERE TO ASGARDIA, YOU'D STILL BE ROTTING ON THE BOTTOM OF THE SEA IN MIDGARD.
MIDGARD...
MALEKITH AND THE FROST GIANTS...
FATHER, HOW LONG HAVE I BEEN OUT? WHAT HAS HAPPENED TO THE EARTH?!

YOUR ALL-FATHER ODIN CARES NOT. MIDGARD IS NOT OUR--
BLOOD.
ICE.
ELVES.
SKULL.
SKULL.
BLOOD.
DAMNED BIRDS. I SHOULD HAVE YOU BAKED INTO A PIE.

NEVER MIND THE ARM. WHERE IS JARNBJORN?
SOMEONE... BRING ME MY AXE.

I THOUGHT YOU MIGHT SAY THAT. BUT I WILL NOT HAVE THE HEIR TO MY THRONE FUMBLING ABOUT LIKE A COMMON CRIPPLE.
YOU HAVE BEEN SLEEPING FOR MANY HOURS, THOR. LONG ENOUGH FOR ME TO SEND WORD TO THE FINEST BLACKSMITHS IN ALL THE REALMS.
I AM TOLD YOU KNOW OF THIS DWARF.
AYE, HE KNOWS SCREWBEARD, SON OF NO-EARS, SON OF HEADWOUND.
SCREWBEARD OF DYNAMITE DWARVES OF SKORNHEIM MOUNTAINS. SWORN BROTHER OF THOR IN LEAGUE OF REALMS.
HAIL, GOD OF THUNDERS. SCREWBEARD BRING GIFT FROM DWARVES OF NIDAVELLIR.
AR

SCREWBEARD BRING NEW ARM. BETTER THAN PUNY OLD ARM.
FORGED OF BLACK URU IN SAME FURNACES WHERE WAS BORN MIGHTY MJOLNIR. TOOK THOUSAND DWARVES TO POUND INTO SHAPE.
EVEN AFTER ALL STARS TURN TO DUST...WILL STILL BE THIS ARM.
YOU HONOR ME, SCREWBEARD.
YOU'VE COME AT A DARK HOUR, MY FRIEND. I'M AFRAID THIS IS NO TIME FOR MEAD.
AYE, SCREWBEARD DOES. NOW TRY ON ARM, SEE IF STRONG ENOUGH TO LIFT MEAD. SCREWBEARD THIRSTY.
NOT WITH MIDGARD STILL IN PERIL. I MUST GO AND FIND MY GOATS.
THOR...THERE ARE THINGS THAT HAVE HAPPENED SINCE YOU FELL...THINGS YOU SHOULD KNOW BEFORE YOU...
NOT NOW, FATHER. IT WILL HAVE TO WAIT UNTIL AFTER I'VE--
YOUR HAMMER HAS GONE MISSING.
WHAT?
AND SO HAS YOUR MOTHER.

NOW.
ROXXON ISLAND.
YOU HEARD ME, WOMAN. WHOEVER YOU ARE.

THAT HAMMER DOES NOT BELONG TO THEE.
THOR...? OH MY GOD, HIS ARM...
I UNDERSTAND YOUR CONCERN, SON OF ODIN, BUT THIS...IS NOT THE TIME FOR SUCH A DISCUSSION.
THERE IS NO DISCUSSION TO BE HAD. PUT DOWN THE HAMMER, THIEF. AND THEN TELL ME...
WHAT HAVE YOU DONE WITH MY MOTHER?
YOUR MOTHER?
AHEM.
THIS SEEMS LIKE A RATHER PERSONAL MATTER, BEST SETTLED BETWEEN PEOPLE OF THUNDER. PERHAPS THE MINOTAUR AND I SHOULD WAIT OUTSIDE.
IT'S MY ISLAND. PERHAPS YOU SHOULD ALL GO TO HELL.

YOU ALSO HAVE SOMETHING THAT BELONGS TO ME, ELF. I WILL DEAL WITH YOU IN A MOMENT.
WE SHOULD DEAL WITH HIM NOW.
MALEKITH HAS MADE A PACT WITH THE FROST GIANTS. THEY WERE HERE SEEKING THE SKULL OF--
I WILL HEAR NO MORE WORDS FROM YOU, PRETENDER, WHILE YOU STILL HOLD WHAT IS RIGHTFULLY MINE.

YOU NEED TO REMAIN CALM, ODINSON. I AM NOT YOUR ENEMY.
THEN WHAT ARE YOU?
I AM STILL TRYING TO DISCERN THAT MYSELF. I JUST KNOW THAT THIS IS NOT THE FIGHT THAT YOU WANT.
FIGHT? DID YOU JUST SAY YOU WANTED A FIGHT?
NO, I SAID...

CALM THYSELF DOWN.
TAP

YOU.
DARE.

I WILL TAKE THAT HAMMER!
WITH YOUR ARM STILL ATTACHED IF NEED BE!
I SAY THEE NAY.

FIRST YOU STEAL MY HAMMER, NOW MY WORDS AS WELL?
I HAVE SOME WORDS FOR YOU, ODINSON.
"WHOSOEVER HOLDS THIS HAMMER..."
"SHALL POSSESS THE POWER OF THOR."
UGGH!
THE POWER OF THOR... BELONGS ONLY TO THOR!
GAAH!
THOOOM
AND YOU ARE NOT HE!

YOU HAVE LOST YOUR AXE, PRINCE OF ASGARD! YOU ARE UNARMED! ASK FOR QUARTER AND IT SHALL BE GIVEN!
DO I SEEM UNARMED TO YOU, GIRL? TO HEL WITH YOUR QUARTER! AND WITH YOU!
ANGRY LITTLE WORMS, AREN'T THEY? IF WE STAY OUT OF THE WAY, MAYBE THEY'LL KILL EACH OTHER.
WHERE'S THE FUN IN THAT?
WE SHOULD BE FIGHTING THESE GIANTS, NOT ONE ANOTHER. BUT ONCE AGAIN YOU ARE LETTING YOUR RAGE GET THE BEST OF YOU, THOR.
YOU KNOW NOTHING OF ME, WOMAN!
ARE YOU CERTAIN OF THAT?
UNHAND MY HAMMER!

I DID NOT ASK FOR THIS! THE HAMMER CHOSE ME!
YOU BEWITCHED IT! WHAT MANNER OF SORCERESS ARE YOU?!
I AM THE GODDESS OF THUNDER!
YOU ARE A BLASPHEMY! THERE CANNOT BE TWO THORS!
YOU WILL NOT FRIGHTEN ME WITH THUNDER! I COMMAND THE LIGHTNING, TOO!
COMMAND IT ALL YOU LIKE! YOU HAVE NO IDEA WHAT IT MEANS TO WIELD MJOLNIR! WHAT IT COSTS!
I WOULD DIE FOR THAT HAMMER! I HAVE DIED FOR IT! AND I WILL DIE AGAIN THIS DAY IF NEED BE!
OPEN YOUR EYES! YOU CANNOT HOLD ON TO SOMETHING YOU'VE ALREADY LOST!
I AM THE ONE HOLDING THE HAMMER! WHO ARE YOU?!
WHAT MAKES YOU SO WORTHY?! WHO ARE YOU BENEATH THAT MASK?!
I AM THE ONE WHO WILL NEVER LET IT GO!
KRAKA-KOOOOM

UNNH!
AARH!
MJOLNIR...?
ODIN'S BEARD...
I HAVE NEVER SEEN IT...DO *THAT* BEFORE.

YES, THAT'S IT.
COME BACK TO ME, OLD FRIEND. COME BACK TO...

THOR...
I TRULY AM SORRY.
IN ALL OUR YEARS TOGETHER...IN ALL OUR MANY BATTLES...
MJOLNIR NEVER FLEW LIKE THAT FOR ME.

YOU HAVE BROUGHT NEW LIFE TO THAT HAMMER. WHOEVER YOU ARE...YOU ARE CORRECT. IT HAS CHOSEN YOU.
HE'S SO SAD. I HATE TO SEE HIM LIKE THIS. I JUST WANT TO HUG HIM. DO SUPER HEROES HUG EACH OTHER?
JUST TELL ME ONE THING...

ARE YOU MY MOTHER?
I KNOW THAT SHE IS MISSING. AND I SENSE SOMETHING OF HER NOBILITY IN--

STILL THINK I AM YOUR MOTHER?
I...
CERTAINLY HOPE NOT.
THOUGH WE HAVE MET BEFORE, HAVE WE NOT? FROM WHENCE DO I KNOW YOU?
HRRR...
I CANNOT ANSWER THAT. BUT...CAN YOU TRUST ME? AT LEAST LONG ENOUGH FOR US NOT TO DIE HERE THIS DAY?
NO.

BUT IT WOULD APPEAR THE HAMMER TRUSTS YOU. AND I TRUST IN THE HAMMER.
THEN SHALL WE, GOD OF THUNDER?
AYE, WE SHALL.
GODDESS OF THUNDER.

The hammer sings its song of thunder.
A song I have heard countless times before.
But never quite like this.
I am Thor Odinson.

Asgardian. Avenger. Prince of the realm eternal.
I am destined to live until the end of time. To wear a crown and sit on a throne.
Or so the stories would have me believe.
But with every giant that falls this day...
With every rumble of thunder...
With every roaring note of the hammer's song...
I die.
I die a little more inside.
And the more I die...
The harder I swing the axe.

WELL THEN, THORS, I WILL BE THE FIRST TO ADMIT...
THIS WAS NOT ONE OF MY MORE SUCCESSFUL ENDEAVORS.
BUT DO NOT THINK FOR ONE SECOND, DEAR LADY, THAT THIS ENDED WHEN YOU SMASHED THE SKULL OF LAUFEY.
THE SKULL OF LAUFEY?
AND TELL ME, MALEKITH, WHAT IS TO STOP ME FROM ENDING YOU RIGHT HERE AND NOW?
I WILL LEAVE YOU TO ANSWER THAT FOR YOURSELF.
THE DULY ELECTED KING OF SVARTALFHEIM BIDS YOU GOOD DAY!
LIKE HEL HE DOES.
YOU INVADED MIDGARD.
AH, TECHNICALLY, THE FROST GIANTS DID THAT. I WAS NEVER HERE.
THIS WAS YOUR PLAN. YOU ARE THE ONE SCHEMING TO START A WAR.
I WILL HAVE THAT ARM, ELF. AND YOUR HEAD.
IT WILL BE YOU WHO STARTS ONE, ASGARDIAN, IF YOU LAY SO MUCH AS A HAND ON ME. AND IT WOULD APPEAR A HAND IS ALL YOU HAVE LEFT.

WHAT ARM? I SEE NO ARM.
NO! DAMN YOU--!
HAHAHAHAHAHAHAHAHAHAHA
BURNING MY ARM WILL NOT END THIS, MALEKITH! I WILL MARCH INTO SVARTALFHEIM ITSELF IF I MUST!
YOU DON'T HAVE TO GO TO SVARTALFHEIM, THOR...
BUT YOU CAN'T STAY HERE.
YOU ARE BOTH TRESPASSING ON ROXXON PROPERTY. PLEASE LOCATE THE NEAREST EXIT, OR ULIK AND MY MEN WILL BE FORCED TO TAKE ACTION.

AGGER. YOU AND THAT TROLL HAVE MUCH TO ANSWER FOR AS WELL.
THEY WILL ANSWER. BUT NOT NOW.
WE ARE NEEDED ELSEWHERE, THOR. WE HAVE FRIENDS IN PERIL.

YOU ARE WELCOME, DARIO AGGER, FOR THE SAVING OF YOUR ISLAND AND YOUR WRETCHED LIFE.
NEXT TIME, I ASSURE YOU, WE WILL NOT BE SO GENEROUS.
HMPH. WHAT SHE SAID.

SO ENDED THE INVASION OF THE FROST GIANTS.
MAGES CAME DOWN FROM ASGARDIA TO RELEASE THOSE FROZEN IN ICE.
GODS AND AVENGERS. WARRIORS AND HEROES. FRIENDS...
AND MOTHERS.
LADY FREYJA... YOU WERE FROZEN ALL THIS TIME. MOTHER, WHAT WERE YOU DOING HERE?
WHAT YOUR FATHER HAD NOT THE SENSE OR COURAGE TO DO HIMSELF.
WE MADE A PROMISE TO THE GOOD PEOPLE OF MIDGARD, AND I WOULD NOT SEE THAT PROMISE BROKEN.
YOU LED THE WARRIORS OF ASGARD AGAINST THE GIANTS? TO PROTECT MIDGARD? ALL AGAINST FATHER'S WISHES?
MOTHER...I DID NOT THINK I COULD POSSIBLY LOVE YOU MORE. I WAS WRONG.
YOUR ARM...OH MY SON, WHAT HAS HAPPENED?
THERE HAVE BEEN GREAT LOSSES THIS DAY, MOTHER. BUT ALSO...
A MOST UNEXPECTED ARRIVAL.

WHO IS SHE?
SHE IS WORTHY. THAT IS ALL I KNOW.
WHOEVER SHE IS, SHE SAVED OUR BUTTS.
SHE SAVED FAR MORE THAN YOUR EMACIATED POSTERIORS, CAPTAIN. SHE SAVED THIS ENTIRE REALM.
DOES SHE HAVE A SUPER HERO NAME YET? PLEASE TELL ME IT'S THUNDER-WOMAN. OR THORITA. OR LADY HAMMER PANTS!
I DID NOT ASK FOR THIS. THE HAMMER CALLED TO ME. I DID ONLY WHAT NEEDED TO BE DONE.
PLEASE KNOW, THOR, THAT I NEVER--
NO...
DO NOT CALL ME BY THAT NAME. I AM NOT WORTHY OF IT.
I AM STILL THE PRINCE OF ASGARD. I AM STILL THE ODINSON.
SON, PLEASE...
BUT SHE IS THOR NOW.
WHAT? NO...
THAT HAMMER HAS THE POWER TO DESTROY WORLDS. OR TO SAVE THEM.
CARRY IT WELL.
THOR.

I...DO NOT KNOW WHAT TO SAY... EXCEPT...
AYE.
I WILL CARRY IT.
I AM...
THE MIGHTY THOR.

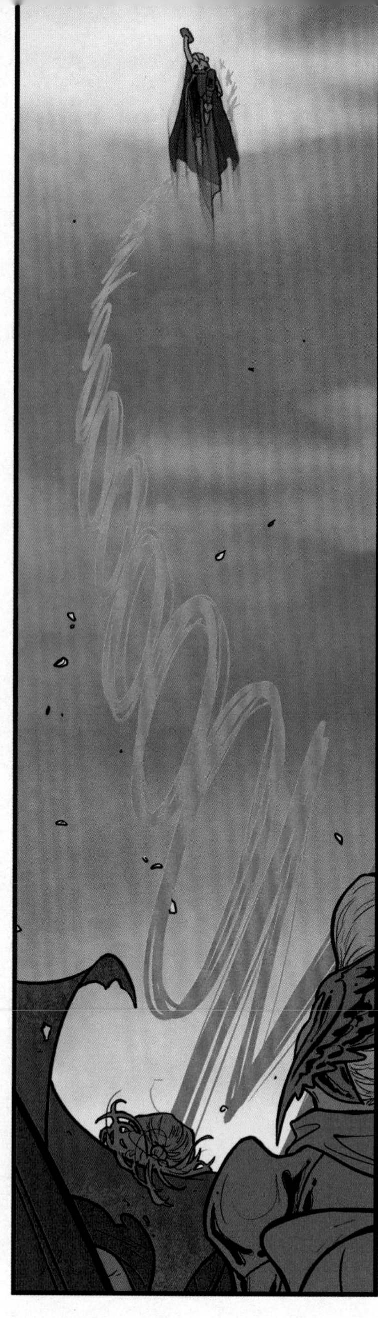

I AM THE ODINSON. I AM THE UNWORTHY. AND THIS IS THE STORY OF HOW I LOST MY HAMMER.
BUT THIS IS NOT THE END OF MY TALE.
YOUR FATHER WILL HATE THIS.
WHICH MAKES ME LIKE IT ALL THE MORE.
THERE IS SOMETHING FAMILIAR ABOUT HER...DO YOU KNOW WHO SHE IS?
NO.

"BUT I LOOK FORWARD TO FINDING OUT."

LATER.
PLEASE EXCUSE THE MESS.
MY LAST MEETING GOT A BIT...OUT OF HAND. I ASSURE YOU, THAT WILL NEVER HAPPEN AGAIN.
I FIND COURTESY IS SUCH A LOST ART THESE DAYS, DON'T YOU? MORE'S THE PITY, I SUPPOSE. NOW PLEASE, IF YOU DON'T MIND, MY GOOD MAN...
WHERE IN THE BLOODY HEL IS IT?

DID YOU REALLY THINK I WOULD LET SOME FOOL WITH A HAMMER SMASH ONE OF MY TOYS? THAT WAS THE DECOY SKULL. THE ONE THE GIANTS WERE MEANT TO STEAL.
THIS IS THE GENUINE ARTICLE. THE SKULL OF THE FROST GIANT KING.

AS FOR THE PRICE, WHAT SAY WE START THE BARGAINING WITH... EVERYTHING I COULD EVER POSSIBLY WANT.
AND WHAT EXACTLY IS IT THAT YOU WANT, MR. AGGER?
REALMS. I WANT REALMS.
AH, WELL THEN...

PERHAPS YOU AND I CAN DO BUSINESS AFTER ALL...

THE UNBEATABLE SQUIRREL GIRL #4

Doreen Green isn't just a first-year computer science student: she secretly also has all the powers of both squirrel and girl! She uses her amazing abilities to fight crime an as awesome as possible. You know her as...The Unbeatable Squirrel Girl! Let's catch up with what she's been up to until now, with...

Squirrel Girl *in a nutshell*

search!

#bankrobbery

#banksnobbery

#mew

#squirrelsuitcrochetpatter

#snackcakes

#squirrelman

G. ALACTUS **GALACTUS** @xGALACTUSx
HEY GUESS WHAT I'M COMING TO EARTH TO DEVOUR THE ENTIRE PLANET

G. ALACTUS **GALACTUS** @xGALACTUSx
AND NOBODY KNOWS BECAUSE I PUT MY SHIP IN A STEALTH FIELD

G. ALACTUS **GALACTUS** @xGALACTUSx
"BUT WAIT," YOU SAY, "AHA! NOW WE KNOW YOU'RE COMING BECAUSE YOU JUST POSTED IT ON SOCIAL MEDIA!!"

G. ALACTUS **GALACTUS** @xGALACTUSx
ONLY YOU AREN'T SAYING THAT BECAUSE NOBODY KNOWS I'M COMING BECAUSE NOBODY FOLLOWS ME ON THIS STUPID SITE

G. ALACTUS **GALACTUS** @xGALACTUSx
...

G. ALACTUS **GALACTUS** @xGALACTUSx
#ff @xGALACTUSx

STARK INDUSTR **Tony Stark** @starkmantony
@unbeatablesg Just heard more of my Iron Man parts have been "borrowed," and now there's a big hole in my building too. Any ideas?

Squirrel Girl! @unbeatablesg
@starkmantony Oh wow dude these suits have wifi in them??? I can go online on my way to the MOON?? Tony ur the best <3

STARK INDUSTR **Tony Stark** @starkmantony
@unbeatablesg That "wifi" works even in Mars orbit, uses proprietary Stark technology, and costs several thousand dollars a kilobyte.

Squirrel Girl! @unbeatablesg
@starkmantony um I already downloaded some songs for the trip to the moon. Sorry!!!

STARK INDUSTR **Tony Stark** @starkmantony
@unbeatablesg Don't reply to say you're sorry! That ALSO costs money!

Squirrel Girl! @unbeatablesg
@starkmantony sorry sorry!

STARK INDUSTR **Tony Stark** @starkmantony
@unbeatablesg Don't reply! Stop replying!

Squirrel Girl! @unbeatablesg
@starkmantony whoooooooooooooooooooooooooooops

Nancy W. @sewwiththeflow
Story time, friends. Your hero, me, thought she'd eat some delicious (cash-only) falafel. So I went to the bank.

Nancy W. @sewwiththeflow
And you know how banks are always the worst even when you're NOT being taken hostage? WELL GUESS WHAT?

Nancy W. @sewwiththeflow
Yep. But then we got saved by @unbeatablesg who appeared in SQUIRREL SUIT ARMOR MODE. Not even joking.

Nancy W. @sewwiththeflow
This really happened. I was saved by a squirrel suit Squirrel Girl. I know you don't believe me.

Nancy W. @sewwiththeflow
tl;dr: doesn't matter, ate falafel

Whiplash @realwhiplash22
I am trapped in #CentralPark and need #squirrelrepellant, PLEASE RT!!!!! #please #rt #please #rt #please #rt

All right! Now to the letters page, and then the rest of this book is just blank pages! Haha, *oh well!!*

Okay, Fine, I Guess It's Not The End.
It certainly was great how we stopped Galactus, Squirrel Girl.
Aw, it wasn't a big deal, Tippy-Toe. The secret's to remember that nobody thinks of themselves as the bad guy, you know? We're all the heroes of our own story, yo!
Hey, we never actually checked. Are the rumors true? Doe every species see Galactus differently or what?
Huh?! Toss me up, I wanna get a good look.
No problem!
Hup!
Well?
I dunno, probably the same way you do. Giant dude, purple clothes, tuning fork hat--the works.
Huh.
So...
...want to go over how we defeated him again?
Oh, sure!!

Yep, that hidden message at the bottom of that earlier page was a lie! Downside: *I'm an unreliable secret message narrator.*
Upside: Hey, at least this comic isn't a total ripoff now, right??

SCIENCE CORNER: You're in space right now, too! You're on a ball of *liquid metal* surrounded by rocks and a thin layer of gas, spinning wildly through the universe at thousands of kilometers per hour. Hang on tight!

If the Power Cosmic is anything like an acorn, *and I'm pretty sure it is,* then we should bury it in the ground and then forget where we buried it and then a Power Cosmic tree will grow from that spot many years from now!

AND LET ME GUESS:
YOU ARE ALL OUT OF NUTS

Basically that's the gist of it, yes.
Also you, uh, you can't eat nuts in space without a special helmet.
Yeah, also, you can't eat nuts in space without a special helmet. I mean, *you* could, *obviously*, since you're Galactus, but, uh...
...but we couldn't.

YOU DO NOT NEED TO REPEAT WHAT THE SQUIRREL SAYS
Frig, no way! You can understand Tippy-Toe??
You can understand me?! *Nobody* understands squirrels! This is *amazing!!*

YES
FOR HE WHO WIELDS THE POWER COSMIC CAN SHOOT LASERS OUT OF HIS EYES, TELEPORT, AND CREATE OR DESTROY LIFE ACROSS ALL OF SPACE AND TIME
SO OBVIOUSLY TALKING TO SQUIRRELS IS NOT REALLY THAT BIG A DEAL

Or she.
WHAT
He *or she* who wields the ower Cosmic can shoot lasers out of his or *her* eyes.

IT'S *YOUR* LANGUAGE THAT LACKS A UNIVERSALLY-ACCEPTED GENDER-NEUTRAL THIRD PERSON SINGULAR PRONOUN
Hey, all the more reason to help affect positive change by being careful about the words you use, huh??
Also, what's wrong with "*they*"?

I DID NOT COME HERE TO DISCUSS LINGUISTICS, I CAME HERE TO KICK BUTTS AND FEED ON LIFE ENERGY
AND I CAN DO BOTH WHENEVER I WANT
BECAUSE I'M GALACTUS

Yes, Galactus can talk to squirrels. He can also fire lasers out of his eyes, and *obviously* by the time you unlock *"Level 1: Laser Eyes"* you've already mastered *"Level 100: Chatting Up Tiny Mammals"*!

EVERYONE WAS ALL "OH LOOK IT'S GALACTUS, I THINK HE'S GREAT BUT THE ONLY WAY I CAN EXPRESS THIS ADMIRATION IS TO STYMIE HIS PLANS, NEVERTHELESS I DO SECRETLY REALLY RESPECT WHAT HE'S TRYING TO DO HERE"

Okay, so the thing is, all my friends live there. I'm sorry... but ***I can't allow you to destroy the Earth,*** Galactus.
I DON'T SEE HOW YOU'RE GOING TO STOP ME
YOU ALREADY TRIED TO BEAT ME UP, REMEMBER

MAYBE THERE WAS SOME MOON DUST ON MY SHOE AND YOU WERE JUST TRYING TO GENTLY AND TENDERLY POLISH IT AWAY
Yes, ***yes,*** that was me trying to beat up a god-tier entity! I'm sorry, all right? It just worked in the past is all.
I beat up Thanos once is the thing.

THANOS
Yeah! You know him? Purple guy? Half goth because he's big into death, but half hipster because he makes his own gloves?
THANOS IS A FOOL

Yeah well, me and Tippy totally beat him up.
And it wasn't a robot, clone, or simulacrum either!

IF YOU SEE HIM, TELL HIM I SAID HE'S SO UNCOOL THAT HE'S NOT JUST A SQUARE...HE'S A COSMIC CUBE

LIKE YOU, SQUIRREL GIRL. YOU DON'T FEAR ME. IN ALL MY TRAVELS, YOU ARE THE FIRST TO APPROACH ME... AS A PEER
I like you too, Galactus.
Me too!

AND TIPPY-TOE, I FEEL FOR YOU. THOUGH YOUR PLANET IS OVERRUN BY HUMANS, YOU AND YOUR PEOPLE ARE ALONE, UNABLE TO COMMUNICATE WITH THOSE YOU SHARE YOUR PLANET WITH. THIS SOLITUDE, THIS AWFUL, ENDLESS SOLITUDE...
...I KNOW IT WELL. YOU ARE LUCKY TO HAVE SQUIRREL GIRL, AND SHE IS LUCKY TO HAVE YOU
Thank you, Galactus.

ANYWAY
I'D BETTER GO EAT YOUR PLANET BEFORE IT GETS TOO STALE
Whoa!
Dude, I thought we were bonding!
WE WERE, BUT A DUDE'S GOTTA EAT
PEACE
Oh man!
Diss!

Turns out you *can't* defeat Galactus by just chilling with him on the moon! All right, Tippy, scratch that off the list, and we'll see how well *"Fight him in orbit **around** the moon"* works out.

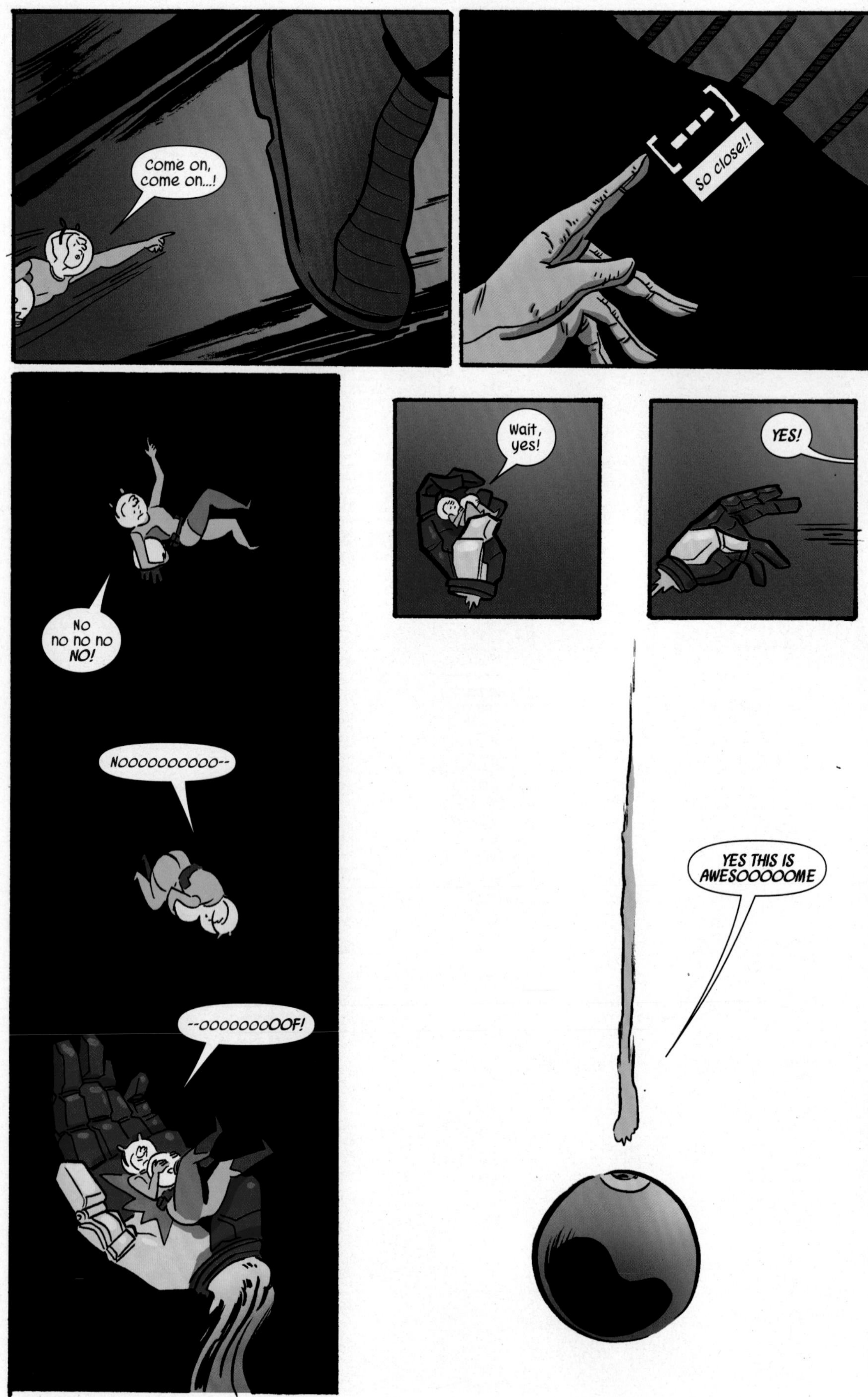

Thanks, Iron Man suit parts! You saved the day. Come on, everyone, let's all give those suit parts...a hand??

Alternate password suggestions: GALACTUSRULES, G@L@CTUSRUL3Z, I<3CONSUMINGALLLIFEENERGY

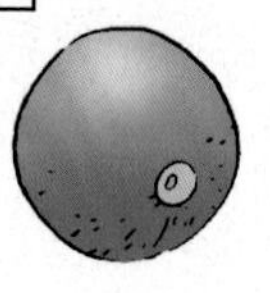

I kept asking myself a question: why would someone who is death incarnate--a force of nature that cannot be reasoned, bartered, or pleaded with--why would such a being come to Earth over and over again, and yet every time--every time--leave without destroying the planet? How are we possibly batting a thousand against him?
Any ideas, TT?
Beats me!

But then I realized, wait a tick: you don't defeat a Galactus by being stronger. You don't defeat a Galactus by being smarter, either. The only way you'll ever defeat Galactus is by giving him what he wants: a source of life energy.
A planet he can eat.
So here's your secret, Galactus: you don't come here to destroy us. You come to Earth because you know we want to live as much as you do, but that we won't trade someone else's lives for our own.
You come to Earth because you know we'll drop everything to find you a planet that's safe, delicious, and not already settled by intelligent life.
You come to Earth because it's the cosmic equivalent of ordering in.

And you *definitely* don't defeat Galactus by having a more audacious fashion sense. Many have tried, all have failed, though honestly many of them looked pretty great while they did so.

SACRILEGE. NOBODY SPEAKS TO GALACTUS THIS WAY. SQUIRREL GIRL, TIPPY-TOE, YOU WILL BOTH BE DESTROYED, WIPED FROM THIS AND ALL OTHER UNIVERSES AND TIMELINES, FOR EVEN CONSIDERING FOR ONE MOMENT THAT--
You could do that, sure. But if you kill us, you won't find the plaaaaaaanet we discovered!
Yeah, we took the liberty of going through your databases, Galactus! And we found one covered--seriously, **totally covered--** with nuts!

NUTS
Oh my **gosh** they're **delicious.** You've never tried one, right? A lot of god-tier beings haven't. I dunno.
Here. Take a look. Examine it with your **cosmic powers.**

THIS IS MERELY AN ORGANIC STORAGE UNIT HOLDING A SMALL AMOUNT OF MATTER
Sure! But examine what's **inside,** Galactus: I think you'll find it's filled with proteins, vitamins, carbohydrates, fats--in other words...

LIFE ENERGY
Calories.
I mean, yes, **life energy.**

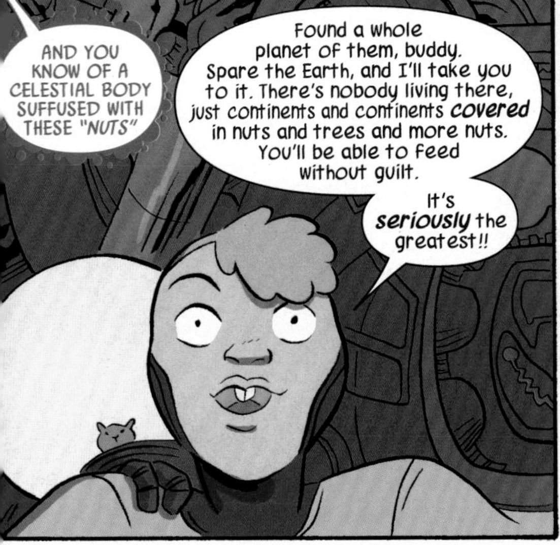
AND YOU KNOW OF A CELESTIAL BODY SUFFUSED WITH THESE "*NUTS*"
Found a whole planet of them, buddy. Spare the Earth, and I'll take you to it. There's nobody living there, just continents and continents **covered** in nuts and trees and more nuts. You'll be able to feed without guilt.
It's **seriously** the greatest!!

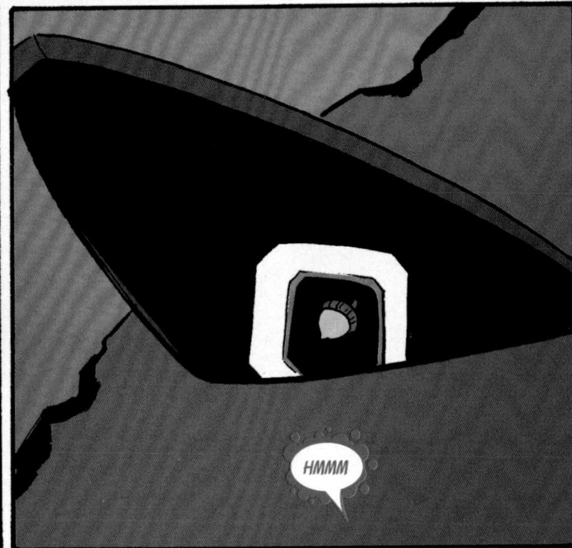
HMMM

Galactus, I don't know what your computers actually look like, but that retro computer interface had ultra-primitive terrible security. Do I thank you, or thank my imagination, or...?

SWOOOF
SWOOOF
On second thought, Galactus, maybe you should eat Earth instead of this planet??
Tippy!!
DUDE, I'M SORRY, BUT THIS PLACE IS THE GREATEST!

So in conclusion, then we came back
the moon to lie down because we all
over-ate, and here we are!
NO REGRETS
Oh, dude, you're awake! Can you send me back to Earth now?
I got class tonight and I'm kiiiinda super late. I could take the Iron Squirrel/Iron Giant-Hand-Thingy but I'm pretty sure I've used up all its fuel by now.
SURE NOT A PROBLEM
BUT BEFORE YOU GO I WANTED TO GIVE YOU A LITTLE SOMETHING
AND YOU SHOULD KNOW THAT AMONG THE MANY POWERS OF HE--
--OR SHE--
--WHO WIELDS THE POWER COSMIC IS THE ABILITY TO READ MINDS
SO I ALREADY KNOW YOU'LL LIKE IT
No way.
No way.
Oh. Oh, Galactus.
I love it.
DEADPOOL'S GUIDE TO SUPER VILLAINS
CARD 1 OF 4522
GALACTUS
- DEVOURER OF WORLDS
- WIELDER OF THE POWER COSMIC
- ...AND A FRIEND
CALL ME IF YOU EVER WANT TO GET INTO HERALDING

Central Park.
SWOOOF
There! Back home with every loose end wrapped up.
SWOOOF
Fly home, Iron Man suit parts! Tell Tony we're even, and also I'm super sorry for the hole I punched in his building!
SWOOOF
Not every loose end's wrapped up, Doreen. We kiiinda left those squirrels fighting the bank robbers, remember?

Oh, dang, the Squirrel Suit squirrels!!

Shortly...
Thank you, Squirrel Man, for saving the day! Any words of wisdom for our boys in blue?
Hah hah! Not the talkative type, huh?
I like it! Keeps the criminal element guessing!!

I won't keep you from your crime-fighting, Squirrel Man! But know this: I, Detective Corson, and my officers, *and* the entire great city of New York are in your debt!

Whew. Okay, *that's* every loose end wrapped up.
Except you're still late for class.

Right. *Ugh.*
I'm gonna have to find a phone booth and *change* in it.

Well, you're almost out of power, so maybe don't fly. Slowly walk or roll home, Iron Man suits!! You're free now!

Oh, don't worry, that's not you! That's my new 100% original character named "Squirrely D. Girly." TRADEMARK AND COPYRIGHT BY ME, DO NOT STEAL!!

Doreen, do you even know where Ireland is? Doreen, do you need to take Intro to Really Basic Geography before you take Intro to Compilers??

Tomorrow's headline: MYSTERIOUS SQUIRREL MAN SPOTTED WITH CAT?? CAT IS NAMED MEW AND SEEMS KINDA SURLY BUT STILL MEGA CUTE.

I swear, animals, you can let me go now. I promise I won't whip *any* of you.
We understand each other, yes?
Hey, you like nuts, I will get you nuts. So many nuts. I will knock over a bulk food store and give you eighty-five percent of the take, yes?? No, no, *ninety-five* percent!
Animals?

Animals, I really really have to go to the bathroom.